NILA
THE BLEEDING GARDEN

a novel

LAILA RE

T0243956

We acknowledge the support of the Canada Council for the Arts for our publishing program. We also acknowledge support from the Government of Ontario through the Ontario Arts Council, and the support of the Government of Canada through the Canada Book Fund.

Cover Design by Sabrina Pignataro

Cover Photo: GN / Drawing vector graphics with floral pattern for design. Floral flower natural design. Graphic, sketch drawing. freesia / Shutterstock.com

Author photo by Purple Tree Photography

Library and Archives Canada Cataloguing in Publication

Title: Nila the bleeding garden : a novel / Laila Re.

Names: Re, Laila, author.

Identifiers: Canadiana (print) 20220271666 | Canadiana (ebook) 20220271682 | ISBN 9781774150856
(softcover) | ISBN 9781774150863 (EPUB) | ISBN 9781774150870 (PDF)

Classification: LCC PS8635.E213 N55 2022 | DDC C813/.6—dc23

Printed and bound in Canada by Coach House Printing

Mawenzi House Publishers Ltd.
39 Woburn Avenue (B)
Toronto, Ontario M5M 1K5
Canada
www.mawenzihouse.com

FOR MY NIECE NILA AND NEPHEW ARMIN

And in memory of my beloved mother

MESSRIE RASHIDIE

1952-2010

This being human is a guest house.
Every morning a new arrival.

RUMI

Contents

Acknowledgements

My mother, a journalist and avid reader who inspired my love for reading. My father, for having the courage to lead and protect his family from war in Afghanistan. He did whatever he could to get us to a better life and education. I want to thank novelist Dennis Bock for teaching me how to start a novel. This novel would not have been written so confidently without his lesson. I also wish to thank Mawenzi House for choosing to publish and believe in my work. Special thanks to my editor MG Vassanji for his close reading of this novel. It was a childhood dream of mine to write a novel because of how much I loved reading novels growing up.

Preface

I lost count of how many times I cried while writing this book. It was a therapeutic and cathartic experience—this is what brought me into creative writing in the first place: healing through the arts. It brought me closer to myself and more understanding of who I am. Besides believing in the power of prayer, it is creative writing that has also been a source of empowerment from the challenges of life. I enjoyed sharing my love of Afghan culture and the opportunity to learn more about Afghan history during the writing process.

I have always wanted to write a novel ever since I was a little girl. I read stacks of novels during my summer breaks. I could read through an entire novel in one day, which allowed me to finish dozens in the span of weeks. It is a dream come true to have finally written a novel that can contribute to the amazing world of storytelling, especially a story from an under-represented voice.

Once I understood how to best start a novel, I began writing like a machine, I was unstoppable and the story came to me so naturally. I was passionate about writing with my authentic voice as an Afghan woman who has experienced first-hand the devastating impact that war and displacement has on families everywhere. I became very attached to my characters and cried with them throughout the writing of this novel, especially because much of it is based on real-life experiences.

The characters represent real experiences of Afghans, including my own, which I witnessed, or heard or read about from the wars in Afghanistan. I believe it is best to learn from the consequences of war—not to turn away from or normalize them.

May all humans live in peace and love.

Choose peace and love.

Introduction

IT HAS BEEN YEARS *since all of the traumatic experiences and tragedies, but here I was on my bathroom floor with the lights shut off and door closed to escape reality. I sat in its darkest corner with my hands against my face to quiet the tears. I wanted to shut out the world in hopes of feeling only God's presence. I was screaming inside but the world could only hear my silence. I needed some privacy and did not want anyone to hear my despair. I grew up putting the needs of others before my own. Betraying myself had become the norm in order to please others, to appear to be perfect and to perform life with a mask on. I was tired of pretending that everything was okay. It was not. It hadn't been for so long. I was in a state of perpetual grief and loss. It's okay to not be okay, I repeated to myself.*

There was a wounded child that existed deep in my subconscious who needed to be loved and nurtured. "Speak kindly to her," my psychotherapist would say. "Speak to her as you would to any other child." I had a lot of anger and shame against the little girl I once was. I did not see her as worthy of the bare minimum since she grew up mostly without it. Violence, neglect, abandonment, and abuse were all experiences that made up much of my childhood memories.

"Nila, you need to be comfortable with your shadow and darkness, just as much as your light. It is a part of you that you can use as a lesson, you don't need to resist or remove it—integrate it in order to know wholeness." My holistic psychotherapy sessions had been very helpful but the memories they brought up and the difficult truths I had

to accept were still more of a burden than a blessing.

I had to re-learn that my mind and body were working with and for me all along. My negative thoughts were survival responses in a toxic environment where my boundaries were not respected and where I learned to not honour my intuition. I was ready now to move into alignment and begin the journey of replacing the negative beliefs with wiser ones through the loving practice of positive affirmations. I knew I was healing not only myself but my ancestors before me and the generations after me.

Breaking the generational trauma was going to have to start with me.

Baghlan, Afghanistan

Spring 1995

MY HEART BROKE THAT night when we left our family home in Kabul, our first home together as a family. I remember our last evening there before we escaped to the farm in Baghlan, about six hours north of Kabul. My father woke us up in the middle of the night and led us outside. We stood there while he disappeared into the dark, gathering things quietly to put into our car. All I remember is objects. Everything felt empty and lifeless. My home became a house. I was losing my connection and meaning to it. There was no chance to say goodbye. For a long time afterwards there would be no chance to say goodbye to anything. Everything seemed to get stolen from me—by the time I could love or become attached to it, it was gone. Everything around me was fleeting and temporary. To me the value of my life became worthless. Anything would be better than this misery, I thought.

The farm we moved to and lived on was our temporary home. It was small and had belonged to my late maternal grandfather. There were other such properties in the area but we did not see much of our neighbours or know anything about them.

⌐

The sun was shining bright upon the wheat field and I was enjoying another morning exploring the farm by myself. My parents were inside the house, consumed by responsibilities. I was a wild and aware five-year-old girl, not enrolled in school yet. The children who went to school were older and seemed like totally different creatures. To me, every day felt like living on the edge. Would I make it out alive by the end of the day? Our lives were too chaotic for anyone to explain what was going on, why I was here and who I was. I had to figure that out on my own.

The wheat field appeared golden, whimsical, and magical today. But like all things in life, there was its other side. It made me fearful. As I wandered inside it, I felt vulnerable and small. The wheat stalks were taller than me, the field looked endless. I felt lost in an endless maze of wheat. I was being slowly overwhelmed by it, it was trying to bury me. This duality of nature raised conflicting emotions in me. I began to learn to enjoy it cautiously. It kept me alive, because it was the source of our food, and yet I felt it had the power to destroy me.

I was constantly in a state between feeling safe and unsafe. When you go from a peaceful, loving life to find yourself away from home amidst a war, nothing can feel certain or stable anymore. Change was always a constant. At a very young age, I became used to uncertainty and instability. My need for control was the product of this condition. I saw the world in terms of controlling my relationship with it. The notion of surrender was lost very young. If I could get lost in the wheat field forever, imagine what the world in its entirety could do to me. I was determined to create my own destiny and sense of things ever since my nightmares began about the overwhelming wheat field. I would wake up in sweats and panic and my mother would bring me a warm glass of *sheer-chai-boora* ("milk-tea-sugar" in Dari, a dialect of Farsi.). This drink was a remedy for many things. I would say "*sheer-chai-boora maykhauyum,*" I want milk-tea-sugar, and my mother would appear like a doctor with medicine. The warm and sweet beverage would calm me down and truly felt like medicine after those nightmares. With every sip, I felt the wheat field growing smaller and I would feel my body grounding itself again. Although she would bring me the remedy, I never actually told my mother about the content of my fears and nightmares. She already had enough fears of her own, and I didn't want to burden her with mine. I also thought that if I spoke about my fears out loud, I would risk hearing an answer that I was not ready for. What if the world was as scary as I dreamed it to be? I kept my nightmare to myself each time it came and sat at the kitchen table drinking my sheer-chai-boora, hoping the enormous images of the wheat stalks would disappear with each sip.

Later on in the morning, my sister Ruby and brother Abdullah would find me playing with the chickens. They were both older than me. People would say that Abdullah and I looked nothing like each other. Abdullah was tall with bright blue eyes, light brown hair, and pale white skin. He got these features from our mother's side of the family. Afghanistan has a rich variety of ethnicities due to invasions by Persians, Arabs, Mongols, Greeks, British, and others. Ruby and I didn't look very alike either. I had olive complexion, brown eyes, and dark brown hair. Ruby had hazel eyes, white skin, and long, jet-black hair. I would often hear people complimenting my mother about how beautiful her children were.

My mother would be dismissive about this. She would say that character was more important than looks. We were also all different from each other in our characters.

Ruby was seven and Abdullah ten. I was the third and last child in the family. Despite being older, Ruby and Abdullah were unsupportive about my fears. In fact they both seemed to reinforce my feeling about how dangerous and deceiving life was. Perhaps it was their way of coping with the trauma of our displacements, but they were troublemakers for me. Sometimes I saw my father raising his voice at them outside the house, his hand raised. We knew that he was very angry when the lines between his eyebrows folded deep; he even had a permanent wrinkle there, perhaps from being angry with them all the time. They were usually punished for stealing something. Whenever I spent any time with them, it would almost always end with me in tears. Somehow they would cause an accident and I would end up hurt. But they were my siblings and there was no way of avoiding them. Every day I would hope that I wasn't going to get my eyes poked or snack stolen by Abdullah. And I tried not to get into another fight with Ruby; this seemed the only way she knew how to communicate.

I would wonder why my siblings were so rambunctious, why my dad was always angry, and why my mom always worried. My father, Abdul Ahmadi, would have his usual serious face on and my mother, Ariana Ahmadi, would look zoned out and depressed. Their world had collapsed. How badly, we would find out in the coming months. On the farm, things seemed to be getting worse for us every day. There was a major change about to come in our lives and I was just waiting for it to be over in the hope that change would make things better. Wondering when things would get better for us and for me was the underlying theme of my days. I hated being inside our house because the reality of being ignored and forgotten amidst angry conversations between my parents made me unhappy. The walls felt like prison walls. I liked being outside, exploring freely and away from these grown-up problems. I thought I could be helpful to my parents by at least staying quiet and out of the way.

One day Ruby started to chase the chicks on our farm. I was nervous about her hurting herself. My parents were busy. Ruby always seemed to be getting into accidents and near-death situations. Every accident seemed to me worse than the last. Previously she had fallen from the roof and then later into a ditch. These were only more traumatizing visions to add to my memories. In an instant our lives could change if one of us were to get hurt seriously. I don't think either of my parents had had any previous experience with young children. They looked just as lost and confused as I was.

My mother was losing touch with her femininity, something she had valued very much—she went from being happily married and provided for, always fashionably dressed while pursuing her passion in news journalism, to struggling to support the family, with three children under the age of ten.

Ruby was laughing and enjoying herself chasing the chicks around the farm. She was friendly to me today. Abdullah was acting like a guard on a power trip—walking around, watching for any chance to scold us. The chicks were the cutest little things. I enjoyed playing with them when I was not walking in the wheat field or running around the farm.

I admired my father. I looked up to him. Even though he came across as a very firm dad, he was the king of the household to us and I deemed myself as one of the princesses. He had promised to build me a dollhouse. Amongst all the chaos of our lives, my relationship with my dad was the most comforting thing I had. He was tall, strong, and fearless. I felt protected and loved by him. I would occasionally ask a question in a soft, gentle whisper. I was not a talkative child. My siblings did enough damage to make me lose any confidence in speaking up or voicing my opinion. I was excited to see him this afternoon to ask him about the dollhouse. He was usually free during the afternoon, when he would take us up to the rooftop of the guesthouse on the farm, called a *baum* in Farsi. Many homes used their roofs or *baums* as terraces. My siblings and I would run around the roof under the blaring sun hitting the cement, and enjoying the view of the village. This would be my chance also to ask him for updates on my dollhouse.

"Nila!" my mother shouted across the farm as I was playing with the chicks. *Niiilllaaaah* is how it sounded whenever she called my name. It always had a frustrated and tired tone under it. "Nila!" She was looking for me. I was confused as to why she was still home at this hour. I was always surprised to see her. It was a rare sighting. She was always busy making a life out of what was left. She had big dreams and was not going to let this impending civil war ruin them. She grew up financially well and struggle was not in her experience. Her father was a businessman who had owned a lot of land. She was very close to him and spoke very highly of him. When she decided to pursue university in the city, he supported her. He would often pick her up from her dorm and take her out to dinner to catch up with her. She earned a bachelor's degree in journalism from Kabul University and was a symbol of a modern professional woman. The future was becoming more hopeful and exciting for Afghan women. I loved seeing photos of her before she was married. She and her friends had the most stylish and elegant outfits. One of my favourite photos of her showed her outside her office building wearing a knee-length black skirt with a fitted turtleneck top and black shoes with heels. Another was of her hanging out with her friends wearing oversized black sunglasses, bell-bottom pants, and a safari jacket. She was ahead of her time in fashion. She was a physically gorgeous woman from head to toe with intelligence, confidence, and ambition. Silky dark brown hair, bright brown eyes, high cheek bones, and full lips. She carried herself like royalty. She married much later than most women because she enjoyed being single and was focused on her education and career. My father, who was an established man and a decade older than her, impressed her with his independence, masculinity, and charm. He was a CEO and owner of a fitness-training company and a boxing gym in Kabul. My mother worked in the same office as his brother, who introduced him to her. He loved to talk about how he showed up at her office one day to meet her and handed her a love note. My mother smiled and declined his offer to drive her home.

He then visited her parents to ask for her hand in marriage. When they married, he provided her with a wonderful wedding when she was adorned with a lot of gold jewelry and wore three bridal dresses. They left the wedding together in a car that was adorned with beautiful white flowers all over and music blaring, which is a tradition. He also provided her with a house, which increased her savings significantly. My father would always boast about how well he took care of her. It brought him a sense of pride and boosted his ego to be able to provide for her. They were truly in love and the talk of the town. A Kabul love story. I believed in romantic love because of them.

"Nila!" she called out again, looking for me. I thought to myself that maybe my dollhouse, which my father had promised to make for me, was ready. The surprise was

finally here! I had stayed quiet and patient about it, not
wanting to bring it up even though I was getting worried. I
trusted that my father would keep his word. I had full faith
in him. I saw my father as pure and perfect, someone who
could never hurt me but would only protect me. A person
whose being held my heart. I was a daddy's girl. "Nila!"
again. My mother was relentless. "Nila, mother is calling
you!" shouted Abdullah. "Why are you ignoring her! Go!"
I put down the chick that was in my hands gently and got
up. The sun was bright, so I put my hand above my eyes to
look for my mother. She spotted me and started waving her
hand.

"Nila!" I ran up to her. She looked tired from walking
in the heat. "Nila, I need you to come with me to meet
my friend in the city. She is a teacher." I was thrilled,
even though this had nothing to do with my dollhouse.
I had never met a teacher or been inside a school. I did
not know how to read or write in Farsi and was eager to
learn. My childhood had been such a rollercoaster for my
parents, dealing with the political turmoil during and after
the Soviet occupation of Afghanistan. It had been endless foreign interference, proxy war, and invasions. Now it
was news of a civil war, riled up by mercenaries, who were
mainly funded by foreign forces. Gulbadeen is the name I
heard often among grown-ups. He was the first boogeyman
I had ever known, behind much of the violence and terror
in the city. I hated that name and that man. I had never
met or seen him, but I knew he was a real-life monster. I
was introduced to the reality of violence very young. News

of death, torture, and destruction never stopped coming. It was my playful childhood spirit that kept me going. The world was dangerous, but it was still a playground in my eyes.

"Now go say goodbye to Abdullah and Ruby before we go," my mother pleaded. She needed me to always be the better person. Appearances were becoming more important to my mother than reality. She cared more about what other people thought of me rather than how I was feeling. Abdullah and Ruby were a bit behind academically for their age, but my parents did not have the resources to understand what their issues were. Our family was being held together by strings. I grudgingly went back to Abdullah and Ruby, said "*Khuda hafiz!*" God bless, and ran off.

Mother held my hand and walked me to the front of the property, where our cab was waiting and ready to go. She sat me in the back with her and told the driver to head for Kabul English Learning Centre. English? I am going to learn English? That sounded very exciting. My mother studied English in university and I heard her speak it sometimes. She was always challenging herself and thinking of the future. I was thrilled. It felt like a privilege to have a teacher to teach me anything. I was imagining someone who cared enough to help me grow and learn while I just sat and absorbed it all. I loved this image of being a student.

Once we arrived in the city, I heard all the noise from the market and the streets. It was busy. There was a lot going on. The driver went into a residential area and into an alleyway. Behind a concrete grey building was an entranceway for the learning centre. There we met a slim lady with a hijab, and she stared down at me with a warm smile. "*Salaam, Ariana. Jaan, chetor astain? Chiqa khoob asta ke shumara meebunum. Chiqa dayr shud,*" she greeted my mother with a bit of sadness. Hello Ariana dear, how are you? It's so good seeing you. It's been so long. They hugged and kissed cheek to cheek three times.

She took us up to the roof of the building for a private chat. Looking out into the city, she explained how bleak things were becoming and her plans to leave eventually. I thought I was here to start my first day but it seemed to be more of a meeting with my mother and her friend. A gloomy one. As they spoke, I began to wander around the roof and soon found myself standing on the edge. I could see way down into the alleyway, into the gap between the buildings. My mother was too busy to notice that I was getting myself into danger, but I thought the better of it and headed back to her. I was confused about what was going on. Was I starting school? Is this just a meeting? Someone please explain why I am here. Suddenly, the conversation was over and we went down the stairs back to the front of the school.

There were kids playing in a small playground that had a circular swing, like a mini Ferris Wheel. My mother was still busy talking, so I went to the swing. There were two other kids there. I felt a bit left out but I was enjoying this amazing swing of a kind I had never seen or played on before. The other kids wouldn't speak to me and seemed to be waiting for me to get out and leave. I slowly turned and made my way out. I looked back and it seemed the kids were laughing at me. I hated this experience. I wanted to leave immediately. I stood by my mother again and she was finally ending the conversation for good this time. They said goodbye once again as the cab arrived. My mother seemed disappointed by the meeting, as if she was losing hope. School seemed impossible because it was unsafe. I stayed quiet and accepted the fact that I wouldn't be going to school anytime soon.

The next day, I was out in the fields again, exploring. Spring was almost at an end and summer was finally approaching. In the summer, my mother usually bought my sister and me summer dresses with matching hats. I wasn't in the summer photo the previous year with Ruby and Abdullah, because my mother said she couldn't find a dress my size. Ruby's dress was so pretty. It was white with a puffy skirt and she wore a big white sun hat and the cutest golden slippers. I couldn't wait to be in this year's summer photo. My mother loved to take and develop pictures, but it was becoming more expensive. She needed a newer camera and it became hard to find somewhere to develop the films, as many businesses were shutting down. I was, as usual, just hoping for the best.

Abdullah popped up out of nowhere. "How was school?" he asked.

"Are we going?" I looked at him angrily. "We aren't going to school. The woman told mother that it wasn't a good idea to come back to the city. She's leaving soon too."

Abdullah's face dropped. He was ten years old at this

point and had lost more years of school than me. I could see the anger boiling in his eyes. He and Ruby were being bullied by some kids from neighbouring farms. They were older so they were judged even more for having or knowing less. He ran off before he could show any further emotion.

Abdullah was starting to have more trouble expressing himself. One day he would be interested in being helpful, then the next day he would be causing havoc. His personality and mood were unpredictable. I don't think it was good for the mental health of any of us not to have had a routine for several years now. There was no stability or predictability in our lives. It started making more and more sense why Ruby and Abdullah were the way they were. Always angry and acting out. They had it bad for longer than I did. I still had one more year before I was to start first year of grade school, so I was not as behind as they were. I felt sorry for them. We were all just trying to survive and make sense of things. I went about playing on my own the rest of the day. The farm was very quiet. It felt like no one wanted to be disturbed with whatever they were doing.

But as the days passed, things did not seem to be getting better, and the tension of waiting for something to happen was suffocating us. We were not able to celebrate Now Roz (New Day) or the last day of the festivities. Now Roz celebrates the first day of spring in the solar new year. A few years of civil war had already passed. My parents did not want to leave their homeland like the rest of their friends and family. They loved Afghanistan. They loved their careers. They loved the lives they had built individually and together. That life was all they knew. There is so much loss and trauma that comes with being forcibly separated from your native land, especially when your lineage extends countless centuries there. My parents would carry this trauma for the rest of their lives.

My parents ultimately did what was best for their children. They realized they could not keep us waiting around on the farm for too long, with no school, toys, or books. Every other day we would receive news that another relative had escaped or that another business had shut down. The people of Afghanistan, and especially the middle-class families of Kabul, were leaving by the droves to safer countries. Kabul was becoming a ghost town left behind for those who were too poor to escape.

I suddenly found myself again being moved without a say or a goodbye. I went to bed at night and woke up in a van with my family around me. My parents must have carried me out of my bed while I was sleeping, because all I could hear and feel was the van speeding over a bumpy road in pitch-black darkness. It was happening all over again. Everything was gone, the life I had known ended abruptly just as I was getting settled and attached to it. The sense of danger was more acute this time. The uncertainties were even greater. I'd never seen my parents so scared. My father was usually fearless, but he looked defeated and helpless. He did whatever he could to get us to wherever we were headed that night.

I saw my maternal grandmother Bebe Jaan and maternal aunt Khala Latifa in the seat in front of me. They had arrived from Panjshir Valley in the night to go with us. Panjshir, "Five Lions," is where the maternal side of my family descends from. It is about six hours south of Baghlan. I have many relatives there that I have never met. Bebe Jaan didn't like city life and had stayed back in the valley where she was born and raised. She loved communal-living and knew everyone in her village. Now she was with us, escaping. I knew it was Bebe Jaan in front of me from her white hair peeking out from her *chadar*, and the blue face tattoos on her pale, wrinkled white skin. She was always a mystery to me, especially her face tattoos. Khala Latifa looked pale and distressed, with her long black braided ponytail that went from a side of her head to her waist. We were suddenly all together heading fast into the darkness. We were fleeing in secret. The civil war must have escalated. My parents had got us out before we risked being killed or abducted. The ride continued, uncomfortably bumpy. We were in the mountains for sure.

The driver of the small bus taking us to the Pakistan border was arguing with my father, he wanted to pick up other passengers; my father was saying he would pay more for him to continue and not stop. We couldn't trust picking up just anyone, my father had his three children in the car and would not risk bringing in any strangers who could harm us. He promised to pay for every empty seat in the bus. We had to get to our destination, Peshawar, Pakistan, before sunrise, a six-hour drive if the bus could make it to the Torkham border crossing. He was counting on this old bus and its driver to get us there directly. I didn't know who we were hiding from or in fear of exactly. I feared he might be Gulbadeen. The hate in my heart grew bigger for him and anyone like him that night. I closed my eyes and went back to sleep, trying to forget what we were enduring and not to think about what was next. All I could hear were whispers of *duas* from my grandmother, praying for us to survive this escape. *La ilaha illallah muhammad ur rasulullah. La ilaha illallah muhammad ur rasulullah* . . .

I found myself awake in the mountains in my father's arms. He was tired and so was everyone around us. We were on foot and they all looked like they had been walking for days. Every step seemed painful. We were very high in the mountains on rocky paths. As if the physical challenge and the uncertainty weren't stressful enough, along our way we saw men wearing long white turbans, with guns dangling to their sides or held in their arms and pointed at us. I did not understand if they were protecting or threatening us. That was my first sight of a gun. I gulped in fear seeing these men. They had so much power and control over us, brandishing those guns so close while we were fleeing with whatever we could carry. I needed to pee and I asked my father to please take me to the bathroom. My father was scared to stop in front of these men and did not want to catch their attention. He paused and held me up in the air and told me to pee like that in front of everyone as we walked. One of the men with guns was bothered seeing this and asked my father what he was doing. My father anxiously replied "Please, I need to help my daughter. There is nowhere else to do this. Just give me a moment." I was embarrassed and terrified at the same time. Once I was finished, my father had to keep carrying me in his arms. I was too frail and little to make it through this journey without help. He was our hero and our protector. It may have been the last time I saw him this strong. The journey was breaking him with every step.

Night came and I had not seen my mother or siblings. All this time I was with my father, hidden in his arms. I could hear him talking with some men at what seemed to be a border. It felt like an entry point. I felt some relief coming over me, for I understood that we were close to leaving Afghanistan. The Torkham border guards were wanting identification and asked if my father was carrying any photographs. They kept questioning my father as if he were in the government or military. This was very scary because he had to lie and hope he was believed. He had had experience with the military as a young man. Luckily, they believed him. I did not know at the time that photographs were banned by the Taliban, a designated terrorist group backed by Pakistan, who were planning to forcefully take over the government of Afghanistan and violently occupy the country.

I later found out that my parents had hidden their photo albums in secret compartments of our luggage. The Taliban wanted to take anything that brought joy and dignity to Afghans. As if smiling was a crime, especially by a girl or a woman. My parents also feared that if the Taliban knew their professional backgrounds, they would be detained. I couldn't understand why these men were so cruel and evil. The sad thing was that they could be found across the border too. We were finally allowed to cross the Afghan border into Pakistan. I was in a new country for the first time. I hoped that things would be better for us here. I was glad the last two days of hell on earth were over. We were safe from war, but I could not take that for granted ever again. My father then paid for another bus to take us to Peshawar which is the closest city from the border. From there, we took one last bus to our final destination, Islamabad, the capital city of Pakistan.

Islamabad, Pakistan

Summer 1995

I WOKE UP IN the morning while we were arriving at an apartment in Islamabad. It was a busy area of the city, located in a neighbourhood that my father referred to as G-9-1 or Karachi Company. There was no fear or gloom on anyone's face. People were going about their business, life seemed to be flowing and at peace. The roads were paved, and I could see stores across an entire strip. Above them were apartments with huge balconies. It was exciting to look at my new neighbourhood. There were many cars, bikes, and motorcycles parked on the street. Children were playing by the trees on the sidewalks. "This is good," my father said out aloud. My mother nodded in agreement. It seemed congested but that just meant there was more to explore. The stores were run mostly by young men with brown skin and mustaches who wore their traditional clothing of long tops with matching bottoms. The women were also dressed traditionally and in hijabs. Mother had some fitting-in to do—she was raised without a *chadar* and was comfortable in western clothes. Things seemed just as conservative and strict here as they had become in Kabul.

My father had managed to rent the apartment, but he

was angry about the rent. Just as we entered the place, there was a letter on the floor waiting for us with bad news. The landlord, named Amar, had raised the rent. "*Chee nooshtas?*" What is written? my mother asked worriedly. My father's expression said it all. He began cursing and yelling. "*E sag! Amar! E khar!*" This dog! Amar! This donkey! The rent was twice as much as the market rent. My father had spent most of our savings to pay for our safe escape. This was distressing. The Pakistani landlords were taking advantage of Afghan refugees by charging them higher than normal rents. They were not welcoming but exploitative of the vulnerable Afghans. Many of them ended up in refugee camps, which were in horrible conditions, with barely any humanitarian assistance available. My father was experiencing discrimination for the first time, in his own neighbouring country by fellow Muslims, when he was at his weakest. My parents had to immediately figure out how to continue affording the rent and not ending up homeless. This left a bad taste in us. We knew now that we would never feel welcome here, and living here would be short-term. I knew not to get comfortable or get my hopes up. It was only a matter of time before we would have to escape this place too. My parents were busy making ends meet in the meantime while figuring out how to move to the West. Iran was our neighbouring Islamic country but discrimination against Afghans was just as bad. Most of our extended family had permanently settled in the West.

My father would be walking furiously back and forth throughout the apartment rubbing his head in frustration.

My mother sat with her hands over her eyes in despair over fears and worries about becoming homeless with her small children in a foreign country. They were facing challenge after challenge. Right when she thought things would be normal, another problem arose. This is when I understood that my life was solely about survival; there would be no kindness from anyone. No matter how good you are, you are on your own on this Earth. While you are here, do not ever expect kindness. Once I accepted that fact, life made sense. Life had showed no kindness to us. It was our hard work and smart decisions that got us out of hell many times. If we had waited in Afghanistan, our life would have proved over and over that there was no kindness there. We were not about to wait on the kindness of Pakistani land-lords or the government to treat us right and fair. You can pray for guidance, but you must ultimately save yourself.

From that day onward, my parents remained busy in their struggle for our survival, and trying to get us out of there to a better life. I did not expect to be able to start school here. My siblings and I continued to wait for better days, trusting our parents to make school happen sooner or later.

"Nila!" my mother called just as I was waking up. "Nila, watch Ruby and Abdullah. We will be back soon," she shouted down the hall before shutting the door behind her and leaving with my father. They left in a hurry early that morning. We all slept on *toshaks*, stuffed seating mats, in one room as a family. It felt good for all of us to be together in one room. It was a two-bedroom apartment but the other room was left empty. We had no furniture but the *toshaks*. Ruby and Abdullah were still asleep. I got up before they did. I had no dolls or books and had only one outfit to wear. I could not read and still dreamed of getting my first doll. I knew the time would come and when it did, I would be the happiest little girl in the world.

The extra bedroom was huge and it had a balcony connected to it. Then there was the long hallway down to the bathroom and living room. As I went along it, I heard curious noises in the living room. I peeked into it and there was Bebe Jaan with Khala Latifa. My khala had her butt and legs up against the wall and her head on the floor with her eyes rolled back, staring at me. Now I understood why my mother left me in charge. Bebe Jaan was busy taking care of her daughter, who was mentally ill at the time. I am not sure what was wrong with her, but the trauma of war and our escape may have disturbed her even more.

Bebe Jaan never spoke much to me or my siblings. She was a woman of very few words. It was a mystery why she did not speak to her own grandchildren. If I asked her a question, she left me even more confused with her answer. She would look at me and hurry me off with *"Buro,"* Go. I closed the door shut and stayed away from them both. We were all under the same roof and I was sure my father wasn't happy about this situation either.

He seemed to have had a bad relationship with his mother-in-law from the start. Apparently she hadn't approved of my mother's choice of husband. At the time, many people would marry within their extended families, because they knew them best. My mother married a *baygauna*, a stranger. It was a risk she took over marrying one of her second maternal cousins. And so the awkwardness in the apartment was ever present.

My mother never explained to me the reason behind Khala Latifa's odd behaviour and antics. We just kept our distance and let her be.

The day was starting and it was my first in this new country. I was excited to make some friends. I had seen a lot of girls playing outside in front of our building the previous day. They were more approachable in this city than the ones in our neighbourhood before.

Kids were biking, running, or just hanging out in groups. Some were helping their parents in their stores after school. I was hungry but all that was left for us was naan, which we ate in the bedroom. I was longing for a feast of kofta and chicken kebobs and chapli kebobs. I missed our family holiday dinner parties. We hadn't had kebobs in months. I grabbed a piece of naan and went out to the balcony for more people-watching. The balcony had rod railings, through which I could see. Below me directly was the entrance to a variety store. The customers would look up to see what this little girl was doing alone staring at them. I would smile back. I didn't speak their language, Urdu, which is similar to Punjabi and Hindi. I wondered how I would go exploring now that I lived in an apartment in a big city, when I didn't fit in at all. The only thing I had in common with the other kids was religion. I was hoping that maybe during the Eid holidays I would make some friends. I started realizing how boring it was going to be in this apartment.

"What are you doing here?" asked Ruby. She had woken up and had come looking for me.

"Nothing," I replied.

"Where are Mother and Father?" she asked.

"They left earlier in the morning. I don't know where, but they said they'd be back soon. They left us naan for breakfast. It's in the bag in the bedroom."

Ruby left in search of the naan. Then she came back crying.

"Abdullah took all the naan and won't give me any!"

Abdullah liked to take everything he could. He would even take my milk bottle in the past and lock me out from the bathroom. He loved to torture us. He always boasted that he was the first child and wished we had never been born after him. Everything was perfect until we were born. This was his recurring reminder to us. It was hard to trust and love someone who wished you were dead. I got up and went back inside the apartment.

Bebe Jaan was in the bedroom pulling the naan bag from Abdullah. "*Beegee*," Take, she said to Ruby. Ruby put her hand inside the bag and took out a piece of naan. It was dry and hard. We would call such a piece *naan-e-qoc*, hard bread. Then Bebe Jaan told us to come into the living room and have some chai with it. We followed her into the living room. She sat beside the *tarmooz*, tea pot, with some tea cups. "*Beegee*," she said as she poured a cup for each of us. We sat there sipping our tea and staring out the living-room window. It was facing another apartment. A well-off Pakistani family lived there. I could see their beautiful furniture.

A little brown boy appeared. He looked younger than me and was perhaps three years old. He seemed friendly and started waving at us with a big smile. I was happy to know we had a friendly neighbour at least. Once we were done, Bebe Jaan sent us out to go play before Khala Latifa came out from her shower. We got into our sandals and left. We had to go down a flight of concrete stairs and then through a metal gate to get outside the building. Once out, we stayed close to each other. "Let's go that way!" said Abdullah, pointing towards a man sitting across the street. There was a group of people around him, watching, and so we went to see what he was entertaining them with.

In front of him on the ground was a large brown straw basket with a straw cover on top.

The man said something to the crowd in Urdu and pointed to his flute. From his hand gestures he seemed to be saying, "Watch what comes out of the basket!" Then he started playing his flute and moving his head to the music. It was a beautiful, mysterious melody, and as he played it a snake slowly started coming up from the basket, pushing up the straw cover. It was the most impressive thing I had ever seen. It was mesmerizing, seeing the snake move with the rhythm of the music. It was a cobra and it was looking straight at me, I thought. Its tongue would come out and it would bob its head towards us. The man was fearless. He would tap on the cobra's head if it needed to calm down.

The relationship between the cobra and the man was incredible. I never knew that a human and a snake could bond like that in real life. I had never seen a cobra before except in Bollywood movies.

Once the snake was back inside the basket, we turned around waiting for the corn trolley to come by on the street.

In the afternoon Islamabad smelt of delicious food. Aromas came from baking and frying. There were snacks to be had everywhere with trolleys going up and down the road, selling desserts called ladoo and jalebi, and roasted corn and samosas.

"*Jawaree! Jawaree!*" Corn! Corn! Ruby happily shouted. The man quickly pulled one out and began to season it. The corn was red with spice and nicely roasted. He handed it to a man. We didn't have any money, so we just watched and smelled. A couple more customers came and went. Then the man pushed his trolley down to the next block until someone stopped him on the way. We crossed the street back to our side of the street. We had to hold hands because the drivers were fast and careless. There wasn't much traffic safety with proper signs, so getting hit was highly likely and you had to be extra cautious. We then went up to the variety store in our building. It was full of treats. I knew Abdullah and Ruby would get themselves in trouble. They loved candy and this store was full of candy for kids. I told Abdullah right away, "*Nako!*" Don't. My father's temper was getting worse and worse. If he was humiliated by the storekeepers due to theft by his children, the two of them would be severely punished. I knew not to upset my father during this time. However, they did not listen. They went into the store while I stayed outside, playing with a stray dog. Soon they came out of the store and ran inside our building, with their hands full, swinging the gate shut behind them. I was frightened in case the storekeeper punished me, since I was standing right outside his store. I ran back inside the building too, and sped up the stairs behind the other two.

"*Bedow! Bedow!*" Run! Run! My heart was racing, thinking about the storekeeper possibly coming after us. We ran quickly into our apartment and shut the door. A minute passed, then Ruby and Abdullah opened their hands. "Look what we got!" said Abdullah. This was not going to be worth our father finding out.

The next evening, that is exactly what happened. The store owner yelled at my father about his kids stealing from him. My father was furious. I was in the bedroom on the point of falling asleep when my father came in and called Ruby and Abdullah out. The door was left slightly open so I could see them in the hallway under the light. I wish I hadn't. My father pulled out a whip and started whipping their legs. It was terrible. My mom pushed my head down and told me to go to sleep. She knew I was sad and scared. It felt wrong and excessive. At that point, I knew my father had lost control. The trauma had gotten to him and he was passing it down. He was not the protector I had known. I was afraid, thinking, would he do that to me? My siblings were screaming and crying. My mother lost herself as a mother. How could she let him do this? I began to resent

them both. I had to sleep with anger and fear in my heart. I
could do nothing to make him stop.

I never witnessed this when we were in Afghanistan or
maybe I was too young to be aware. Maybe this was why
Abdullah and Ruby were so aggressive and often out of
control. My father was displacing his rage onto them and
my mother was neglectful. When and why did she stop
caring? Who was to blame? Whom should I hate more? I
was buried in questions and silent tears. A sense of despair
was planted within me. That moment made me accept
and normalize dysfunction very young. How could I ever
ask anyone for help, when I could not find refuge in my
own country, in my home, with neighbours or parents? My
world as a child was set on a stage of despair.

The next morning began another day in our quiet,
empty, gloomy and grey apartment. There were still no toys
to play with or books to read. It would be another day of
sitting around and staring at the world. I always felt like
I was waiting for something and often ended up waiting
alone. This feeling of anticipation and incompleteness was
the reality of the limbo we were living in, in Islamabad.
It wasn't home and would never be home. So where was
home? And when would it arrive? My only understanding
of home at one point in time was Kabul. I held on very
tight to this delusional idea of us returning to Kabul, which
caused me to live in denial and in the past. This was too
much for me to have to understand on my own at such a
young age. The days flew by living in my mind. My imag-
ination was a whirlwind of ideas on how to make it out

alive in this world and anticipating what was next. I always had to be ready because I did not want to feel as lost as I was now. There was some sanity in living in your own world—at least you knew who was in control and no one could reject or neglect you. Any time you were confused with questions, you just made up the answers.

Finally something exciting happened early one afternoon. Father came home with a television! We were in Bebe Jaan and Khala Latifa's room sitting around idly on the *toshaks* when he suddenly burst through the door with a TV in his arms. It was small, with a long antenna sticking out on its right side. Ruby, Abdullah, and I got up quickly and gathered around our father, who was holding this thing we had only noticed in the stores. I remember my parents having a smaller one in their room in Afghanistan, but not sure if it ever worked. It always had grey static whenever it was on. We used to listen to radio for news and entertainment on my father's black stereo. It was quite impressive, hearing people and music come from it, but the television was even more impressive!

I wondered about all of the things we could possibly watch on it. It was an exciting moment. Suddenly we forgot about the rough night we all had and our anger towards our father. He placed the TV on the table in the corner of the room beside the entrance, facing the window, and plugged it into the outlet there. We sat down on the floor in front of it and waited for it to show something. To our disappointment, it was that grey static again. My father began to turn the dial on the top right corner of the TV while moving

the antenna around. "*Aycheez naysta!*" There is nothing! we
began to complain. My father fiddled with it a bit more and
suddenly a cartoon appeared! My first cartoon ever. It was
a mouse and a cat chasing each other in a show called *Tom
and Jerry*. We were so thrilled, in spite of the static and the
black-and-white picture. There was another cartoon called
Road Runner. It was my favourite. The bird would outsmart
the coyote each time in such a clever manner. It was hilari-
ous. The rest of the day we watched whatever cartoon our
signal could catch. Later that evening, my parents joined us
in watching a silent comedy with Charlie Chaplin. It had us
all laughing. We did not need to know the language or culture to connect with it. It was very human. And it was the
first time in a very long time when we enjoyed something
together.

Most of our days now were spent sitting in front of the
TV. It was a brilliant invention for our parents to keep us
in one place and out of trouble. It worked magically. We
would sit quietly together enjoying cartoons and sometimes
the occasional Bollywood movie. Everyone was enchanted
by the famous, beautiful actress of the time called Sridevi.
We watched an older film featuring her called *Nagina*,
where Sridevi was a cobra in human form. Just like the
cobra and the snake charmer we had seen outside performing for bystanders, Sridevi was the cobra possessed by the
sound from a musical instrument. The culture here was
very much intrigued by cobras and had integrated them
positively into society. I was introduced to so many different narratives and images—Indian, British, and American.

From Charlie Chaplin to Sridevi to Mickey Mouse, the world seemed more fun, connected, and so creative.

I was becoming comfortable in the community, even though from a distance, like a tourist. We went to a circus one day. There was lots of entertainment there and food; there were rides. My mother had bought us all matching grey sweat-suits with Mickey Mouse on them prior to the fun day.

Things must have gotten financially better for my parents because they began to give us presents. I was excited to wear my American outfit. It was brand new and had the coolest cartoon on it. "*Bya, ax e ton beegeerum,*" Come, let me take your picture—my mother pleaded for us to gather for a photo. I was so excited about the photo that I forgot not to stand by Abdullah. While my mother was preparing to take the photo, Abdullah was grabbing at my face and then poked me right in the eye. That photo moment was ruined and I started crying, my mother couldn't take another photo with my red eye.

During our walks through the fairgrounds, at one point we heard the sound of loud engines and saw a large group of men gathered in a circle. I made my way to the front and looked down upon a steep and wide circular hole. Two motorcyclists were riding around against the walls of the cavity, passing each other as they went up and down. There were small cars parked too, waiting to join. It was as thrilling to watch as the cobra I had seen dancing out of the basket. The people in this country seemed to be casually fearless dare-devils who were not worried about death but had complete trust in God. They were happily living on the edge; in the streets passengers would stick their bodies out of vehicles. The casual nature of it all was what was so astonishing to me. That lack of fear did rub off on me, for I was looking forward to riding a bicycle one day as freely as those motorcyclists. I left the circus feeling a bit braver and bolder.

Days went by and we watched countless episodes of cartoons each day. We didn't have an understanding of what the future held for us but we trusted our parents. Until then, we settled for whatever life we were given. There were no more complaints from us. We got used to our way of life as wild, wandering children. It was obvious that our parents were still working hard towards moving us out of Pakistan. My mother wasn't comfortable or happy living here for the long term. She had been going around on her own as a journalist in Western-style business clothes in downtown Kabul, now she had to go about in conservative, traditional Pakistani outfits with a male accompanying or driving her. Even then, the harassment against women and girls was constant. She did not want Ruby and me growing up here, especially as Afghan girls. Besides that, there was no chance of citizenship for us here. We were foreigners and refugees. I was hopeful because a departure always seemed imminent. I often heard my parents saying to each other *"bayat dars e khoob beegeeran."* Must get a good education. That was the most important thing for them in all their efforts—to give us access to the best education and a bright future.

In my brave moments, I would try to start a conversation

with Bebe Jaan. I would point at her face tattoos and ask her what they were. "*Khaal asta*," It's circles, she said, "*rasum asta*," It's drawings. The tattoo ink was a bright blue. She had an upside-down triangle in the middle of each eyebrow with about two *khaals* inside. She had more *khaals* on the sides of her eyes, each with three dots forming a triangle. They were a bit faded due to wrinkles and aging but still uniquely beautiful. I wanted to know more, but that is all she would share. She would close her lips tightly and retreat into her own little world again. Another time, I wondered what happened to her husband, my maternal grandfather. I remember him once staring down at me in Kabul inside our house. He was a tall, dark, and handsome businessman—also strong, serious, and powerful. I asked her about this while waiting in the hallway behind the door. I don't remember who we were waiting for but it was a great opportunity to finally ask about his whereabouts. "*Kooja asta agha jaan?*" Where is grandfather? She looked at me, perplexed. She was not expecting that question. She gave herself a few seconds to come up with an answer. She bent down to whisper to me in her dry, crackled, and deep voice.

The story went something like this: she was walking with him when a stairwell appeared in the sky on which he began walking up until he disappeared into the sky. This story amazed me with its magic but also scared me. I kept wondering why she didn't stop him and then I imagined myself running after him. As usual, Bebe Jaan left me more puzzled and confused when I asked her a question. From then on, I tried to figure out where these stairs were and where he disappeared to. Could he see me from above? I would visualize him walking peacefully and innocently up these long stairs, light from the clouds shining on him. It kept me busy just imagining where he went and feeling sad why no one stopped him. I would have stopped him.

I woke up one day to a very quiet apartment. It seemed cold and abandoned. There seemed to be no one home. Then Bebe Jaan appeared before me. She knew I had woken up. I must have been asleep when everyone set off somewhere. "*Kooja?*" Where? I asked looking around. Something serious must have happened. She bent down to my eye level and softly said "*Maudarit shafa khuauna ast,*" Your mother is in hospital. I didn't remember what had happened the previous night. I had fallen asleep early. Something must have happened to her after I fell asleep. I must have slept through it all. My heart ached inside. I felt cold and weak. My heart was flying away in the air like a lost balloon. I sat there on the dim, cold empty hallway floor. I was going to wait there. Then Ruby came out into the hallway too and sat down beside me. "*Ba chee mintazir astain?*" What are you waiting for? she asked. "*Maudar,*" I replied, Mother. "*Kooja asta?*" Ruby asked.

"*Shafa khana.*" Hospital, I said.

And so we both sat down in the hallway for the next couple of days waiting for her. Days turned into a week. A week turned into a couple of weeks and then into a month. It was the quietest and saddest time in our apartment. We didn't know what had happened to her and when she was coming back.

A month later, as we were watching TV, Bebe Jaan returned smiling from a phone call and told us "*Maudarit myaya*," Your mother is coming. We stared out the window waiting to see a glimpse of her as she got out of the car and came up the stairs to our apartment. To finally see her face. We hadn't heard from or seen her in over a month and not much of our father either. He was away working during the day and visiting her in the evenings. He didn't talk to us or explain what had happened to her. It was a fragile situation, and they did not want to speak of it but only to pray about it. Then finally her face appeared! There she was, our mother coming up the stairs with the help of our father and Bebe Jaan.

Each one was at her side holding her arms. She looked thinner and weaker with a bandage around her head. Something had happened to her head I thought. My happiness turned into sadness in an instant. What if she has forgotten me? My heart, wherever it was lost flying, probably burst now. Its pieces fell on the ground in front of me. I've lost my mother I thought. And I swallowed the lump in my throat as she approached the door. Life was becoming heavier and heavier. She slowly walked into the apartment and was taken straight to the new single bed in the empty third room to be left alone. There was no hello or acknowledgement from our mother. She just passed by us like we were strangers. Whatever was left of my heart was probably irreparable at this point. I was shattered and shaken. I was a little girl unrecognized by her mother after a month apart. I needed her warmth and love more than anything

else. I was her youngest. I ran into the bedroom in tears. I
did not understand her condition, no one had explained or
prepared me for this. All I knew was that my mother didn't
miss me like I missed her. It was unbearable.

I don't remember much of the rest of the day except
for angrily isolating myself from everyone, the door to my
mother's room shut all day. I bent my head down sitting
outside the interior balcony facing Bebe Jaan's room. The
window there was open and I could overhear her speaking with my father. "*Yaadish raft archeez mayga. Khow bood taw
dee show,*" She's forgotten everything, they say. She's been
asleep since last night, my father said. My mother had been
in a coma all along. She had been in a car accident while
sitting on the passenger side. A car had crashed into them
from behind throwing her head against the front of the car.
She had been fighting for her life ever since, in a coma.
The news was depressing but shed some light towards what
was happening. I had to pray now that God would grant
my mother's memory back and hopefully soon. We needed
her. We all needed her.

The nightmares of the wheat field returned. I had
thought they were long gone and left behind in Kabul, but
they continued, followed me to Islamabad. Life was beating me down again and it was the perfect timing for the
wheat fields to mock and overwhelm me. I wish I knew
what they were warning me of, but who would stop to help
me interpret my dreams or even take them seriously? I was
on my own with this battle too. My dreams were a source
of guidance for me, but there was too much missing. It was

a stressful time in our family, so I had to remain quiet in the middle of the night after my nightmares. There was no one to comfort me with sheer-chai-boora. I would just curl up with my eyes closed, waiting for the difficult feelings to pass. I couldn't tell the difference between my nightmares and reality because of how real they felt, as if the world was ready to swallow me whole with the slightest movement. I stayed still, sweating and terrified.

Some weeks passed, and we were in a whirlwind again. Suddenly my mother was back in the hospital. However, this time Bebe Jaan, Khala Latifa, and father were happy about it. My mother was having a challenging year but everyone was grateful she was alive at least. The world was beating her up worse than me. As a struggling mother of three, her life was hard, especially as we were foreigners in the male-dominated society we were in. There was no chance for her to even think about herself for a second. The world seemed to be pulling her apart and demanding every piece of her to submit and serve. She was losing herself, her control over her life. It hurt to see her face looking as if she was spooked all the time, as if her facial expression was frozen with shock and drained of life. Now her body was there but her mind was gone. I hoped she'd return from the hospital in better shape and health. Maybe they would cure her of whatever was distressing her.

I asked Bebe Jaan about where my mother had gone exactly, "*Kooja rafta?*" Where did they go? As usual, she left me further confused. *"Rafta da ko ke shtuk a beegeera,"* They went to the mountains to get the baby. I was completely taken aback. The baby? What baby? Why are babies in the mountains? How far was this mountain? How did she travel up the mountain? How did she choose this baby? Why do we have to pick up a baby? Asking my grand-mother questions raised more questions. I spent the next few hours imagining and contemplating more. I visualized my mother and father walking up a grey mountain with a light on the top where the baby was gifted to them. No one explained how babies were made or even how I was made. I thought that I must have been picked up too somewhere. So we waited impatiently for this baby. A new baby! It was exciting now, wondering if I had a sister or a brother. I preferred a brother whom I could teach to be kinder than Abdullah, and maybe he could challenge Abdullah some-day. Maybe my little brother would take Abdullah's place. I imagined having a sibling whom I would get along with and who would be friendlier to me. Maybe my life would be less lonely. Maybe he would understand me better. Maybe we would have a lot in common. I was becoming more and more thrilled to meet this new baby and my first younger sibling. I had so much love to give. It was almost like having my first doll finally, but a real one.

Then my father came up the stairs, gently walking towards our apartment door, holding something covered in white cloth. Behind him was my mother, her head down and looking even more pale and drained. She had just escaped a civil war, survived a car accident, and was still in recovery from it all—while being pregnant. It must have been the hardest nine months of her life.

My father placed the baby in a home-made crib dangling in my mother's bedroom. My mother went to her bed and lay down for a bit before the baby needed her attention.

Suddenly my father appeared in Bebe Jaan's room, where we were waiting, watching cartoons. He turned on his black stereo and began playing some classical Afghan songs. My father was a charismatic man, and we hadn't seen this side of him in a while. He began to dance, something he was confident about and had a great joy for. "*Dukhtar asta*," It's a girl, he happily announced. The stereo was playing our favourite singer, Ahmad Zahir, who had tragically and mysteriously died very young on his thirty-third birthday. My mother would proudly tell us how he was her neighbour in Baghlan province, where my grandfather owned land; it was their third home. Panjshir province was their first home. Their second home was in Kunduz province. Three northern provinces that were side by side with each other. I don't remember travelling to any of the northern provinces except for Balkh. Kabul province is a central one where I was born, specifically in Kabul City Hospital.

Laily Laily Laily, Laily jaan
Qandol, shereen Laily Laily jaan

was the song playing loudly in Farsi.

Most of Ahmad Zahir's songs were in Farsi, others in Pashto, Hindi, and English. The beautiful sounds of the tabla and rubab enriched the energy of the beautiful moment and filled my soul with feelings of returning home someday. We all sprang up into a silly dance, copying our father's moves but in a restrained manner for Ruby and me. My father had both his hands raised at head level and moved them in and out swiftly. This was the main dance move, your heel and toe going up and down but in a more elegant way for girls and women. This was one of my favourite songs.

The name Laila was very popular and beautiful. It means "night" in Arabic.

Laily Laily Laily Laily jaan, qandol, shereen, Laily Laily jaan,
Laily, Laily Laily, Laily dear sweet cute Laily, Laily dear

We continued to dance to other songs by Ahmad, including, "Sultan e Qalbam" (Ruler of my Heart), "Dostad Darom Hamesha Hamesha" (I Love You Always Always) and "Ay Dil, Ay Dil" (O heart, O heart).

Ahmad Zahir's talent was unique. He brought the deeply poetic Afghan culture into a perfect musical form. It was always bittersweet to hear his music. So much beauty was violently and tragically cut down in Afghanistan. My home and my soul were a bleeding garden. We were dancing roses with thorns. Hearing his music from a time when there was some peace in our lives was both crushing and rejoicing. We spent the rest of the night listening to music and having sheer-chai with naan.

My little sister was not yet named. Bebe Jaan probably

had ideas. She was fascinated with Egypt and wanted to give Egyptian-inspired names to as many of her grandchildren as she could. She had a grandson named Qaira for Cairo, a granddaughter named Mesir for Egypt, and I, Nila for the Nile River. But I had one name in mind: Laila. I went up to my father, who was sitting on a *toshak*. I sat down next to him and knelt my elbow on his knee. "*Bauba, maytonum naum ish kunum?*" Daddy, can I name her? I asked. He replied, "*Maudarit naumish maykuna az khatireh dukhtarasta. Ke bacha maybood, ma mayhaustum naumish kunum. Kudom naum?*" Your mother will name her because it's a girl. If it was a boy, I wanted to name him. What name? "Laila," I spoke shyly. "*Beesyar khoob, eenee nom mayfaumum khush maykuna,*" Very good, this name I know she will like, he smiled.

"Bia ke borem ba Mazar" (Come let's go to Mazar) was the next song—one of my father's favourite. It was an Afghan folk song, referring to Mazar-e-Sharif, the capital of Balkh province and fourth largest city in Afghanistan and known for its beautiful blue mosque. We have a family photo of us standing in front of it. I remember seeing it for the first time with amazement, how grand and shiny it was. My father rose to the occasion now as the song began, pulling my hand up with him. I laughed and began to dance along, covering my face out of shyness. My father smiled as he showed off his dance moves, his very clear facial expressions showing us how much he wanted to impress us. Abdullah, Ruby, Bebe Jaan, and Khala Latifa all clapped along.

My father was very entertaining when he was physically

well. He had been having muscle aches and soreness lately. Occasionally, he would lie on his stomach and ask me or my brother or sister to walk along his back. He would always say that when he was physically well, he could be happily helpful—which was very true. Once one of us was done walking on his back, he would stand up, relieved and grateful. My grandmother, however, would be watching anxiously, fearing that we might injure him.

Once the song was finished, my father decided to entertain us some more with his own vocals.

He wanted to be a singer as a child, but his father, who had bravely moved alone to Kabul City from rural life in Kandahar, was not able to afford music coaching for him. My father now began first with a Gul Zaman song sung in Pashto, the second official language of Afghanistan. "*Oooo watan walo / dabula khushanlee dough / Oooo watan walo / dabula khushanlee dough!*" O people of the country / another happiness has come! He moved on to another Pashto song, by Nashenas called "Mohabbat," (Love). Finally, my father sang Farhad Darya's Farsi song "Dunya Guzaran," (Life Passes). Be happy, old and young.

He loved sentimental songs that called upon the essence of Afghan spirit and the wisdom of life. When there was a problem, he would raise his hands and say philosophically, "*Dunya du roz ast,*" Life is but of two days, or "*Dunya guzaran*"—implying that life is short and temporary. I think this kind of thinking was helping him get through life. I began to say this to myself like a mantra too.

My mother was more into poetry than dance. She was

a very reserved and shy lady. My favourite singer was the Iranian Leila Forouhar. She had hit dance songs in Farsi like "Janomeh" and "Del Ey Del," as well as one in Arabic called "Balady." My mother liked softer and slower songs from Afghan women like Hangama and Naghma. She also enjoyed reading poetry by Mawlana Rumi, who was born in Balkh. It was common in our culture to memorize poems and recite them passionately in a formal dialect.

That day ended beautifully; it was perhaps the best day so far that we had had here in Islamabad.

In the morning, I saw mother sitting in the interior balcony on the swing there with her back against Bebe Jaan's window. I slowly opened the door and pretended to be interested in what Ruby was doing. Ruby was playing nearby with her collection of rocks. I looked down at the rocks while peeking at my mother to get an idea of how she was. She looked tired. She was swinging back and forth gently, breastfeeding my baby sister. "*Eeneera paydau kadum emroz,*" This one I found today, Ruby explained. I was curious if father had spoken to mother about the name I had suggested. Mother caught me staring at her but looked at me blankly. It was hurtful, but I had to remind myself that she was recovering. I still did not have her back, but I did gain a new sister. Life always had its good and bad sides. I chose to remain hopeful and positive. I didn't have the solution, but I would pray that it would come for my mother and our family soon. I left her alone for now and went back

inside to watch cartoons. When my father arrived home
from work, I asked him about my sister's name. He was
very tired but I got the chance to confirm once he walked
in. "*Nomish Laila asta*," Her name is Laila, he said. I was
so surprised and proud to hear this. I had named my little
sister after my favourite singer! Laila was also born at night
so I am sure my mother thought that it was a fitting name.
She also loved "Laila and Majnun," a famous story about
forbidden love.

Our first year in Islamabad was coming to an end. I
was becoming impatient with the limbo we were in. When
would I start my first day of school? How long would we
spend our days wasting away? Where was the rest of our
extended family? Our Islamic holiday, Eid al-Adha known
as the Festival of Sacrifice, was coming and we had no
plans that I was aware of. Celebrations like holidays and
birthdays seemed to have become nonexistent. We were
struggling more and more. It was too expensive to host parties or even to attend any. We were tight on everything—
food, clothing, and gifts. It was our first Eid al-Adha in
another country and away from our homeland. My parents
and the countless generations before them had spent holidays in Afghanistan. Traditions were beginning to break
for us. Every day I felt more distant from who I was and
where I came from. Would we ever return to Afghanistan?
Would we have to move even further from home? Who was
I becoming? All these questions and thoughts were running
through my head.

The nightmares continued except this time they would

also be about stepping into quicksand. I'd seen a quicksand once in a Bollywood film in which soldiers accidentally fell into it during a battle. The fear of a quicksand stuck to me and represented a lot of my growing insecurities about making deadly mistakes and my minuscule position in the world as a little girl. Constantly hearing more bad news than good made me feel that life was always out to get me. I couldn't make mistakes, I needed to be perfect, all-knowing, and have a plan. I had to be several steps ahead of everyone, everything, and the world. I had to know and predict what would happen accurately or it could cost me my life. I was becoming hyper-vigilant, over-thinking, nervous and less spontaneous. Life seemed like trouble and I had to be the bigger troublemaker. *I'll show you who will make it out alive!*

Not knowing that no one makes it out alive anyway—death is guaranteed for us all—I was fighting with fate and life rather than surrendering to God and relieving myself from the impossibility of understanding everything.

I kept my nightmares to myself. I still had no one to confide in about them and no more sheer-chai-boora either.

Eid al-Adha arrived. Ruby and I wore the best outfits we could put together with whatever we had. We also took a red lipstick from our mother's room and painted our lips with it. Ruby and I planned to walk around our block in hopes of receiving treats or gifts from our neighbours. Once we were ready, we ran out laughing, in a hurry to make the most out of the day. There was more music than usual on the streets and lots of people saying "Eid Mubarak," Happy Eid. Ruby and I would giggle out of shyness when wished Eid Mubarak. We would stop, bow our heads and say it back in a lower voice, then run off to find neighbouring children who might share their treats with us.

We ended up at our new friends Fatima and Hamna's house. They were both wearing traditional Pakistani dresses, matching salwar-kameezes and matching scarves around their necks. Fatima was in light purple and Hamna in light pink. They looked lovely and were kind to us. They brought out a tray of sweets which we shared sitting down outside their apartment. After that, we walked across from their building to where there were some trees with shades to play under. We were laughing and chasing each other around when suddenly Hamna stopped. *"Chup!"* Quiet! she said, standing still and staring innocently towards a tree. Her eyes signalled to us to look away from what was behind her. I peeked over her shoulder and saw two men walking up. They looked very similar to the men with guns we had seen when we were fleeing Afghanistan. These two were dressed in cleaner and more fashionable clothes, white with black vests and the same black turbans on their heads with tails trailing over one shoulder. They looked like monsters—mean and angry. One of them had his gun over his shoulder. Owning guns was a common thing in both Pakistani and Afghan society, but people kept them safely indoors. Men were proud of their guns and would even take photos of their infants beside a gun or a child holding one. But these two men seemed above the law and carried them publicly with impunity. We slowly walked across to the other side and off the road and out of their way.

Women and girls were not respected but abused publicly by men like them. They had violent hatred towards everyone but especially women and girls. They did not like to see us playing, learning, feeling confident, or even walking outside. They wanted us dressed in burqas covering us from head to toe with slits cut around the eyes for sight. According to them, women and girls had no rights or freedoms.

I was on the verge of crying but had to be strong so as not to cause attention. They could easily take us away and no one could stop them. Many girls were kidnapped and found dead and tortured in a ditch. Recently we saw in the local newspaper news about four murdered girls lying somewhere, badly beaten. We were terrified and terrorized by these types of men. They were members of Taliban.

Talibs, from the Arabic word for student, were mostly young, poor boys who were brainwashed and trained in Pakistan's madrasas using extremist textbooks produced by America and distributed by Pakistan for waging "holy" wars. These students were vulnerable to abuse and molestation by the mullahs. My father informed us that they were created by the Pakistani government as a proxy force and the country was their support base. Its leadership consisted mostly of Pakistani nationals. Father had told us recently that much of Afghanistan was now occupied by the Taliban and everyone had lost every human right and freedom. He warned us to stay away from them if we ever saw them here in Islamabad. They were enforcing a violent, inhumane way of life and falsely labelling it as Islam

for their political agenda. The secret images and video clips
of what was going on in Kabul showed a living nightmare.
I remember seeing a photo of a boy walking around with
amputated hands tied on strings hanging off a wooden stick.
They had made life a hell on Earth for Afghans, instilling
terror in everyone. They were the antithesis of freedom,
education, and justice. They did not represent my country,
culture, and religion.

We made it safely across the street and hurried into our
friends' apartment hallway. We waited for a minute, then
peered out of the door until we were sure they were completely out of sight and gone. A sigh of relief escaped from
all of us. We felt like we had survived a kidnapping.

Fatima and Hamna told us that it was best that we left
now and made it home safe. We said goodbye and walked
quickly back to our apartment. Our Eid had ended on a
disappointing note. We ended up staying home the rest of
the day and tried to forget what had happened.

Abdullah was out with the neighbourhood boys for Eid.
Apparently some fathers had organized a fun musical ride
around the city in the back of a truck. The truck was quite
full, so Abdullah had been sitting on the edge right beside
the wheels, his feet dangling out. The wheels were large and
had spikes sticking out of their sides. He was not paying
attention and when his left foot swung too close to a spike,
it sharply slashed his ankle, which began to bleed heavily.
Thankfully, my father had been on the scene, seated in a
car behind the truck. He heard Abdullah scream off the top
of his lungs. The truck immediately stopped, and my father

grabbed Abdullah and hurried home.

I saw him racing up the stairs carrying Abdullah. He put my brother down where Ruby and I were hanging out in the hallway. My mother, who was still in recovery, came out looking panicked and faint. *"Allah! Allah! Che shoud?"* What happened? she asked, smacking her hand against her forehead. Abdullah's ankle was a horrible sight to see. The locals, having seen and heard the commotion, brought over their medical kits. They began to apply pressure, cleaned the wound with alcohol, and wrapped it with bandage. Abdullah was crying nonstop, his face red and wet, a mess. He was like a big baby and probably ashamed of himself for getting hurt. We felt bad for him and left him alone to heal. Our Eid turned out to be a calamitous day.

Over the days, Abdullah's ankle began to heal. The pain was going away and he was walking more comfortably. There was a huge scar on his ankle that he became proud of and would show around. It was a pink, thin, transparent skin spread across his ankle. His warrior scar. A mark representing survival. For some odd reason, I wanted one too. Once he was fully healed, he began to walk around confidently with his scar. The other boys began to look up to him for being so strong and he became the leader of his pack of friends. Most of the kids in the neighbourhood were scared of him now. He would stick his chin up as he walked, as if he had died and come back to life. It seemed good news for Ruby and me because everyone knew he was our brother and would not dare to mess with us. We let him be. He had turned tragedy into triumph for himself.

Things were quiet, calm, and peaceful for the next few days. We went about our lives. Father was busy with work. I wasn't sure what he was doing to earn money, but he didn't need my mother's help anymore and it would be wrong to expect her to work after her accident and having a newborn. He would not risk putting her in any kind of danger again. He was the breadwinner and head of the household. He looked proud and confident again. I still saw my father as the King of Kabul. He was royalty in my eyes and I continued to believe in myself as one of his princesses. Mother was at home taking care of her newborn girl and the home. She was busy all day and night. My baby sister was very needy and cried a lot. It was impressive to watch my mother possessing so many skills. She could cook, clean, sew, supervise, write, nurse, study, teach us, and the list went on. In my eyes she could do anything she wanted. My father being able to pay the bills on his own allowed my mother to become a better woman, wife, and mother. She was in her twenties and always maintained and valued her femininity. Besides, Islam protected women by obligating their husband to marry only if they could fully provide for a wife. Otherwise, she was better off single and being taken care of by her parents. He was happy to see her comfortable, relaxed and safe at home with her children. She had gone through enough hardship with the civil war and the displacement. He felt bad about the dangerous, impoverished situation his family was in and was doing everything to make it right again. He was not only a king but a warrior who was trying his best to protect and lead us.

Mother had started to warm up to us as she spent more time recovering and resting at home. She began to get better day by day and soon was her normal self. Her hair was voluminous and curlier again. She began to smile a bit more and dress up in her Western fashion. One day she took a family picture in Bebe Jaan's room holding Laila in her arms. I was surprised to see her do that. I wasn't beside her in the picture but it was nice to take one together. I sat beside my father as usual with my elbow on his knee. I loved to make it known that I was a daddy's girl.

As Laila became less needy, my mother picked up her work again. There were business opportunities here for women in making carpets, clothing, and other things. I saw even Abdullah behind a loom weaving a carpet. It had numerous white strings from top to bottom and you would pull the strings around according to the design. I had no idea how it worked exactly, but it was very impressive to see, and Abdullah enjoyed learning.

One afternoon when Ruby and I came back from playing with our neighbour in his balcony, we saw three looms in mother's room. They looked like long white tables with metal sticks across the middle from one end to other. The room looked like a carpet factory. I was a bit perplexed, but my mother was excited. She had her hands placed on each cheek with a big, bright smile. "*Tashakar beesyar zyaut. Beesyar khoob asta*," Thank you very much. It is very good, she told my father. She was sitting in front of one. Each loom had a bench that could fit two people. My mother must have become very good and confident at weaving.

It turned out that she was starting her own business from home. She spent most of her days in what became the carpet room and office. Afghan women would come to work at the looms with her. I didn't know what they were doing exactly but it seemed like they had a lot of orders. Our home became more lively and prosperous with this business. Father would come home more often with kebobs and other snacks and freshly baked naan after work. The naan would have a sweet warm aroma. We would run up to him to see what he had brought for dinner each day. He would put down his briefcase, open up the plastic bag he had brought and pull out the snacks. My eyes would open wide and my mouth would water. I loved kebobs, especially kofta kebobs, with their rich seasoning, the oil dripping on to the naan. My second favourite was chapli kebob. My mother enjoyed shish kebobs, which consist of chunks of grilled meat, and lamb chops.

We both loved food, especially our authentic Afghan food. Whenever she cooked, she would not forget to mention that it was an authentic *Kabuli* recipe. This is *Kabuli* rice. This is *Kabuli* patty. This is *Kabuli* salad. We were proud to be from the city of Kabul and missed it very much. We were still in limbo, however, we didn't know if we would return to Kabul or go even further away from our native land.

I was beginning to grow tired of wandering round our block and staring out into Islamabad from our baum. I was

almost seven and hadn't started school yet. I should have
been in the first grade and was worried that I would miss
it like Abdullah and Ruby had. They were years behind in
school. I did not want to fall behind or start late. I loved
opening books and looking through them, even though
I couldn't read or write yet. I would take the books from
Bebe Jaan's room and explore the shapes of the words.
They were printed so beautifully and neatly.

I thought to myself that I could print words like that too
if someone taught me. Father and mother couldn't teach me
for several reasons. They didn't know if they should focus
on me learning Farsi, Urdu, English, or Arabic. Nothing was
for sure. They also lost track of time and my age. I don't
think they even knew that I was supposed to start school
soon. I think they just hoped to find the best school for us
and for sure it wasn't going to be in Pakistan. The schools
there still didn't welcome or admit Afghan children. You
had to homeschool or start your own school. My father had
no time to teach, and my mother had other priorities. It
was a very confusing and uncertain time to be focusing on
sending us to a school, and we still didn't feel fully safe in
Islamabad. Everyone was aware of the kidnappings and
trafficking of children, especially Afghan children, who
were vulnerable as refugees. The children were trafficked
for sex and trained as dancers to entertain men. Pakistan
was a strict Islamic country where alcohol and discos were
banned. Men would illegally pay to watch trafficked Afghan
boys dance and rape them afterwards. This was called *bacha
bazi*, boy play. It was my parents' worst nightmare.

They would remind us that it was better that we stayed home than settle for any school where we were going to be either brainwashed, abused, killed, or trafficked. That is why our wandering was limited to our block. We never walked any further. My world was pretty much that block.

One day father came home with a big brown envelope with lots of papers inside. He handed it to my mother immediately and she opened it up to read. They sat down on the bed in my mother's bedroom and workplace. I watched from the door to see what this important document was, anxious to hear good news about what was next for us. Were we finally leaving Pakistan? Was I going to start school in time? Were we going to be reunited with some of our extended family members?

I hadn't seen my favourite aunt in years. Her name was Gulak, which means "like a flower." It was a common term of endearment to call people *gul*, flower. We also call each other with terms like *qalb*, heart, and *jigar*, liver, which in its implication is the same as heart, and even *nafas*, meaning breath; they all represent something that is vital to our existence. Poetry is ingrained in our language. We usually would say *jaan* after someone's name but the second common endearment was *gul* or *gulak*. That probably was her nickname but that's what she went by, Khala Gulak. I heard that she had moved to another land that was even farther away than Europe.

I only knew some things about Europe, which had countries like Germany, Russia, and Poland. My father had visited Germany and Russia once for work and told us great things about life there, but the countries were kafir, non-believers of Islam. It was culturally a very different world from what we had known or seen. They were very foreign and strange to us but still very friendly. My mother had visited Poland once for work and she told me she did not join her colleagues to the disco there after work. She did not want to be dancing in the dark with drunken strangers and it went against her religious beliefs. A very different lifestyle from what we had known.

In our culture, women would not physically or romantically engage with men unless they were married. The only late-night parties Afghans would attend were weddings or engagements at banquet halls that were very formal, with no alcohol of course. And sometimes it was divided by gender depending on how religious your family was. Women and men would have their own party rooms. However, Kabul City was becoming more secular, where mixed-gender wedding parties were acceptable, though it was mostly men and very young children who danced.

"*Embassy deega afta bauyat beraim,*" We have to go to the embassy, next week, my father explained. I didn't know what country's embassy he meant, but that was good enough news. My parents' application to move to another country had been accepted and the next time they would visit the embassy for an interview. I knew my parents would only have picked a country that was better for our future. They continued their discussion in preparation for the meeting. This was a lot of pressure on them. They had to answer questions to prove they were worthy; only a small number of people were accepted each year to immigrate to Western countries. The process also cost a lot of money, and they were putting aside most of their earnings to pay for their applications. It was hard being a grown-up, I told myself, I would enjoy being a child as long as possible, because grown-ups had too many responsibilities and expectations placed on them. I was happy not to have to go to the embassy. All I could imagine was a huge, dark office with an intimidating man behind a huge desk looking at me dead in the eyes and scanning me up and down while asking some challenging questions. I was glad that I did not have to be a part of that. I felt bad, however, that my parents were going to be under a microscope. They were human and had their own insecurities. I just hoped that they knew they were the best and would get through the interview. It was the last hurdle to pass before being granted entry into a developed and prosperous country. This was a very nerve-racking time for all of us. A single decision could drastically change the trajectories of our lives.

I contemplated what I would become if we left Pakistan. Would I become less of who I was, farther away from home? Would moving farther and farther mean becoming more and more lost? Could I bring along everything that made me who I was? How could I remain who I was? Did I need to tell people who I was? Should I be happy or sad? Should I stay stuck in the past and in denial about the future or should I embrace this change and be kind to myself? I was making things harder for myself by questioning, doubting, and overplanning. No one explained anything to me and I would go silent whenever I had a concern. I became powerless when I needed help. I hated this about myself. It was like drowning inside of yourself. Like you're screaming inside but no one can hear you. I was screaming inside at this moment. I wanted to scream, WHERE ARE WE GOING? But I couldn't find my voice. Something in me liked to torture me by taking away my voice when I needed it the most. I had felt a lot of shame from a very young age, but my parents were unaware of this.

Finally, the day came when my parents dressed up to go to the embassy. My father wore his best and only professional suit with his black dress shoes, and took along his black briefcase. My mother wore a long black skirt and a grey blouse and a pair of low black heels. She had on a maroon lipstick. They looked serious, confident, but also a bit worried. They had four young children now relying on them not to mess this up, this chance to get us out of here, so we could get on with our lives. We were ready to be pushed forward into change, even though we had no idea what we would face on the other side. It seemed better than growing up in Islamabad as Afghan refugees. Here, there was no possibility of integration or citizenship for Afghans anytime soon.

My parents left and we all waited anxiously for their return. We were watching cartoons but constantly looking out the window and waiting for a phone call. Bebe Jaan and Khala Latifa did not seem worried as much. Bebe Jaan said that she was going to somewhere called California where her eldest son Aziz lived with his wife and children. Aziz was very much like my maternal grandfather. Very tall, strong, smart, and hardworking, she explained. Bebe Jaan was a grandmother, refugee, and a widow, whose son was in California, so her application was urgent and had a priority. A lot would be changing once our applications were approved; either we would be moving with our bebe and khala or going our separate ways. It all depended on the decisions of the embassies and which country approved us first. Bebe Jaan would possibly leave us behind, I realized. That saddened me. I didn't want her to leave us behind or leave without us. I was now used to her presence and our routine of having chai with her and watching TV in her room, while she prayed. I didn't realize that she wouldn't be coming with us or was not included in our application. We were two separate families on paper. My first six years of life were one big mess; the wheat field was laughing at me every chance it could get, while the quicksand waited for me to slip into my demise. The world was one big bully and I was its favourite one to pick on and torture.

By the time my parents were home, we were already asleep. In the morning, father was off to work and mother was back at her new weaving routine. I guessed my parents had to wait for the decision from the embassy, so there was no news or update to share the next day.

Mother had two other women working with her. All the weaving tables were busy and filled. I wasn't sure how my mother was making money from this business or if she was doing it as a hobby. I didn't understand but it was fun to know our apartment was becoming popular with other Afghans nearby. During lunch hours, some Afghan boys would come and watch the ladies work on the machines. I didn't know if they were there for a break or were waiting for an order. But it was fun meeting new people and seeing new faces. The time would pass with all these visitors to our apartment. They would sit on the *toshak* beside a window and against the wall facing the machines. We felt very important and were doing very important things.

A couple of weeks later my father came home from work with an open letter in his hand, looking defeated. It was evidently bad news. The discussion in the hallway with my mother was pretty clear. He was telling us that our application for California wasn't approved. The reason was something about not having sufficient income to provide for ourselves when we arrived. They did not believe my mother had secured a paid job there, which was required. My mother had mistakenly told the interviewer that she wasn't sure if she would receive income and seemed insecure about employment. This is what I understood. She looked like she had failed everyone. She was a sensitive woman and even more so after the car accident. She began to cry and went into her room and shut the door. Bebe Jaan came out to the hallway to check up on them. She had her hand to her mouth in disbelief. It was now certain that we would be separated from her eventually and soon.

My mother wanted to follow her mother to California. She needed all the help she could get with four children to

take care of. Over the past weeks, Aziz got her excited as he
told her on the phone about how beautiful it was there. He
said he had rented a large house with the help of his two
sons and we could all stay with them temporarily. As well,
there were so many Afghans already there living closely
together in a city called Fremont. It sounded like a better
place for us to move to. But that dream had crashed and
burned with one rejection letter. We needed a new plan.
We were back to square one. California was not meant to
be for us.

As my parents brainstormed another plan for moving, the
days with Bebe Jaan and Khala Latifa with us were coming
to an end. They had quickly received notice of their flights
and were already packing. So much changed and happened in less than a year. My mother had that drained
and tired look again. She was sad about being separated
from her mother indefinitely and not being able to move
us out of Islamabad yet. She also needed help watching us
so she could run her business. It kept her sane and gave
her a sense of sisterhood with the other Afghan women.
It reduced the pain of our disappointment. She had made
a friend in this business, a woman called Jamila. She was
a widow of the same age as my mother and looked a lot
like her. She had a son. Her husband had been murdered
recently by the Taliban at the border-crossing when they
were fleeing Afghanistan. I overheard how they shot him
in cold blood in front of them. The two women supported

each other and my mother was a lot happier. This was a sisterly bond that was not there between her and her real sister, Khala Latifa.

The day came when Bebe Jaan and Khala Latifa were leaving us to go far away. We would not be able to see them anymore. My father carried their suitcases down the stairs where a cab was awaiting them. My mother and Jamila would go with them to Islamabad International Airport. Once all the luggage was downstairs and the cab had arrived, we took one last picture together in the interior balcony. My mother sorted my siblings and me in front with Bebe Jaan, while Khala Latifa stood behind us. My mother stood behind me with her hands on my shoulders, and Jamila took the photo. Laila was asleep inside with my father watching her so they were missing in the photo. I think my father was the only one not affected by the departure. He didn't like Bebe Jaan's interfering ways, and our lack of privacy. Also, my father didn't think it was healthy for us to observe Khala Latifa's odd behaviour. He waved from across the balcony one last time and watched us walk them down to the cab. Abdullah and Ruby weren't emotional about it at all. I was neutral now because I was worried about when we would finally leave this place too! It felt like everyone was leaving for a better place except us. Bebe Jaan didn't have much emotion either, she probably was worried about travelling safely and not getting lost along the way. Maybe they would cry at the airport during their final farewell. I was glad to be staying home because I did not like seeing my mother cry. It was the most depressing and uncontrollable wailing when she started. The only thing that would calm her was falling asleep.

Once the cab drove off, we ran back upstairs quite happy, knowing that the TV was all ours now and so was Bebe Jaan's room. We could watch whatever we wanted and hang out in there whenever. It became our playroom. We would also share the washroom with two less people— Abdullah liked to hog the washroom and play in the shower so now there was a better chance for me and Ruby to use it. We would miss Bebe Jaan's shoula, sticky rice, for sure! She could make the best shoula with lamb, peas, and the tastiest quroot mause—sour yogurt, with onions sizzling on the top. That was probably my best memory of her.

When my mother arrived from the airport, she went straight to her room, wailing as we expected. There was a depressing echo throughout the house. It made us all feel sad inside for not being able to bring her enough joy in her life. We held back our own tears and went our separate ways in the apartment to grieve privately. It was a sad, dark evening.

My mother was soon busy on the phone calling family members around the world for guidance on what to do next and to find out who could help us apply again. I heard names of places such as Switzerland, Germany, Australia, France, Canada, and England. I spent a lot of time at home listening to the calls so as to get an idea of what was going on. She began to say Canada a lot and then it was the only country she would mention on the phone. I didn't know anything about Canada or where it was. We didn't have a map, I had never seen one. I had no clue what Canada was, but it sounded like our next hope. My parents became busy in the evenings with paperwork and talking on the phone with relatives in Canada. There was a lot of yelling on long-distance calls, because the sound quality was not good. There was no way of knowing about this country called Canada even though my parents were shouting its name out every night.

Things began to move fast again once they were decided on Canada. My parents did their best to prepare for a possible meeting with the Canadian embassy. We had been in Islamabad for over a year. Every day spent in Pakistan was a waste of our education, time, and future. My father was now in a panic. I had just turned seven and missed the start of grade one. Abdullah was eleven and falling behind further; Ruby was nine. Abdullah knew his alphabet and numbers in Farsi but could not read well. Ruby and I were still illiterate. Our father told Abdullah to teach us the Farsi alphabet during the day, but he was too temperamental. He would abuse us if we made mistakes, and this made us run and hide from him. The quarrels between Abdullah and Ruby were getting worse. They could not stand each other. Every little thing caused them to bicker. The last fight they got into was over Ruby wearing Abdullah's one and only Michael Jackson t-shirt. It wasn't Ruby's idea to wear it, but my mother wanted a picture of Ruby in it. My mother had to jump in between them to stop Abdullah from ripping the shirt off her.

Mother had no idea how to handle them. But she kept herself busy and productive with work. She continued her business from home while Laila was in the crib nearby. One morning I woke up to a large, brown, wooden office desk in her work room. It was grand and was placed facing the door. There was a cream-coloured telephone in the left corner. Mother was sitting at the desk like an elegant boss, posing with the phone in her hand for a photo with Jamila, as my father held the camera. The two of them looked proud and loved working together. I hadn't spent much time with my mother but was glad she was healthier. Abdullah was awake already and waiting for his turn to join the photo. He stood against the left of the desk with his arm on it and a grin on his face. Then the phone began to ring, and they all got back to work. My father put the camera away and said goodbye before heading off to his work. I still wasn't sure what work my father did, but he was out all day. It was still a time of struggle to pay the bills.

I walked up to the grand desk. It was taller than me and had nice curves on the top. I walked around it some more and noticed two small cupboards on each side. I opened them and saw they were still empty. It was an interesting day of playing around the office desk. I'm not sure where it came from, but it was a nice piece of furniture and made my mother's business look more serious and promising. I wanted to have my own desk someday as a busy woman with papers in front of me. I would hold the pen to my mouth, my head resting on my hand while thinking hard about some problem. I wanted to be a working woman like them.

I finally discovered what my mother was working on so hard behind the desk with Jamila. They were both writers and wanted to start their own women-led newspaper. The launch day finally came, and my father took us all to the launch event. It was my first community event and it was held in a room which had many photos, Afghan dresses, and art on the walls—the kind of things that represented my mother's newspaper. I was walking around the room with many grown-ups towering over me, gazing at the exhibits. One photo was of the four little Afghan girls who were found beaten and dead in a ditch. I was horrified to see them magnified. It hurt to see them. They looked just like me. I stared at the photo, tried to figure out what had happened to them. I was in denial when I heard about them, believing they were alive and just posing, but the photo was so gruesome and made them so real that I couldn't lie to myself any longer. Their clothes were dirty with black marks all over them. Their faces were also stained with dirt as they were probably dragged and thrown into the ditch. I listened to the women beside me talking about what happened. The girls were kidnapped and missing for days until finally they were tragically discovered. My mother's newspaper was a free press that wanted to bring awareness to the plight of women and girls. The lack of safety. The lack of education. The lack of basic rights.

Then I heard my mother's voice on the speaker. The lights came on spotlighting the small stage where she was standing. She began to welcome everyone to the event and introduced all the women who were involved in organizing it. Then Jamila appeared behind her holding a large board with a white cloth over it. My mother pulled back the cloth to reveal the name and cover of their first issue. Everyone began clapping. The newspaper was titled *Azadi*, meaning freedom in Farsi. She read a poem by Mawlana Rumi about being a guest in this life and to be grateful whatever the journey brings. It seemed like she was fully back to herself. Her recital was stylish and eloquent. Afterwards, there were a couple of brief speeches and then everyone went back to mingling. I walked up to my mother and pulled on her long, black skirt.

She noticed me and began to introduce me to the women she was speaking to. Then she pointed to a photo of a baby. We walked up to it and she told me that it was me. I was taken aback, because in the photo I had dark black lines shaped around my eyes, bright white powdery skin, and bright red lipstick. I was confused, why had they done that to my face? She said it was a tradition to wish newborns great health and beauty, and to protect them from the evil eye. As well, there is a recital of the Shahada, the declaration of faith, into the ears of the newborn. Although the makeup looked odd at first, I felt loved and blessed knowing the intent behind it.

The event was beautiful and filled with enthusiastic people. I was inspired by it and especially by my mother. We had a bonding moment over my baby picture, which made me feel special for the first time in a long time. I held it close to my heart and memory. I didn't think that our life was getting better in Islamabad, but my parents were doing their best out of our circumstances.

Lessons at home with Abdullah began to get worse. For some odd reason, I wasn't able to memorize past the first four letters of the alphabet. When he asked me to say them out loud, I would go "*Alif, Be, Pe, Te. . .*" and the rest would just be a blur. I didn't understand why I couldn't memorize the letters or take them seriously. I had very little interest in learning the alphabet. It wasn't like there were books to enjoy once I learned it. Where would I see Farsi words, everything was in Urdu in Pakistan, so even if I could read—the alphabets were the same—I wouldn't know the meaning. "*Aycheez namayfaumee!*" You don't know anything! Abdullah would yell. I would just give up and hide in the washroom for as long as possible. My best trick was to ask to use the washroom and then shut the door and peek out to see if he'd finally stopped waiting for me. Time was the saviour. Eventually he would get bored, forget, and calm down and go off to do something else. He couldn't tell on me because father wasn't home, and mother had left him with the full responsibility. He wasn't being honest with her about my progress because I think he was getting rewarded for helping me. Ruby was even more challenged by the alphabet. Her concentration was weak with everything. She was also very irritable and highly emotional. I wasn't even sure if Abdullah was teaching us right. Why would I memorize something that could possibly be wrong? The uncertainties and instability of our life didn't help us to concentrate either.

One day my father asked him in my presence how my reading was going. I froze. I did not want my father

to ask me to read the alphabet out loud. I was afraid that
he would lash out at me too. Abdullah loved to rile up my
father against us. He pointed at me and said, "*Khud a put
kad da tashnob*," She hid herself in the washroom. My dad
was disappointed that I was skipping my lessons.

"*Bya eeja*," he said, Come here, patting the space beside
him. I sank my head and sat down next to him. He asked
Abdullah to get the alphabet book. Abdullah handed it to
him and my father opened it up and pointed to the letters.
"*Bukhaun*," Read, he commanded. "*Alif, Be, Pe, Te. . .*" I
mumbled and went on mumbling my way as far as I could
into making him believe I knew most of it. I basically made
similar sounds to the noises I could recall. My father looked
confused and disappointed. I thought I could trick him with
random sounds. "*Tauna Alif, Be, Pe, Te mayfaumee?*" You only
know Alife Be Pe Te? father asked. So my plan to trick him
did not work. I nodded my head and tried to save myself
by saying "*Yaud meegeerum*," I will learn. My father looked
at Abdullah, who was grinning, and told him to continue
teaching me. I tried to look interested and eager to learn,
which I think convinced him.

The days seemed longer because of having to endure
lessons with Abdullah in the morning. He continued to
enjoy proving that he was the superstar because I was still
unable to memorize the alphabet. His teaching was more
like mocking. "*Ekha asaun asta*," This is so easy, he would
say. I was still stuck with the first four letters of the alphabet, but I would pretend I was practicing to pass the time.

My new trick was to tell him that I would read it out

when I had memorized it all, or that I memorized a lot but didn't want to read it out loud. I had to find new ways to stop him from getting me into trouble with father. I probably prayed for a way out, I thought maybe this was why Ruby didn't know her alphabets either. Learning from our temperamental and aggressive brother was not encouraging or genuinely helpful. If anything, he was probably stunting our growth by instilling fear and insecurity in us. The less time we spent around him, the better. We avoided Abdullah more and more.

One evening, our parents suddenly took us on a trip to a learning centre. We arrived at a small building, which had one large room where they dropped us off. Inside, a bunch of children were sitting on the carpet with *toshaks* facing a tall, slim, white man with big glasses, wearing a white t-shirt and khaki pants. He was speaking another language and had a stick pointing to a white board on the wall facing the children. Abdullah quickly found himself a spot and was excited to participate. He was the only one who had been to school before, so he was comfortable. I sat in some spot in the middle to get a good view of the teacher. The room was bright with white lights. The whole experience was strange to me, especially since I did not understand a word of what the teacher was saying. He seemed friendly and was smiling the whole time. The other children seemed playful and giggled while he spoke. They began to repeat his words while I sat observing them. It was interesting to be a part of a class for the first time, but I hoped that Abdullah would not be in the same class as me next time so I could learn in peace.

Days passed and we never went back to the learning centre. It was a one-time session.

My days were spent watching cartoons mostly. Abdullah had become busy with mother in helping her entertain her customers. He was very sociable; it came to him naturally. He talked a lot and would even speak over my parents' heads and meddle in their conversations. Our parents did not always like that.

Abdullah would always take my father's side in any argument. But someone had to watch the workers sitting in the weaving room. It kept him away from the street and prevented trouble. It was good to know he was occupied with that. Ruby and I had the TV to ourselves. I would take charge of the TV, adjusting the dial or the antennas if there was too much static. I felt smart when I was able to fix it or find a channel that worked better. And so we pretty much continued to spend our days in front of the TV. Time somehow was flying by with us simply sitting in front of it.

One night something absolutely terrifying happened. I was awakened by screams coming from downstairs and the sound of my family running out of the house. I followed them downstairs to the building entrance. My father was there with another man at the gate, pushing people out. I could see hands sticking out trying to push my father back. There was a crowd of men yelling angrily in Urdu, screaming at us. They were about ten and completely in a rage. I ran towards the gate to help my father. We pushed back the gate as much as possible so it could be locked. My small hands against the gate pushing my little weight against it,

I wasn't sure if I was helping, but all of us together were adding more pressure. Finally, we managed to lock the gate, pulling the long metal rod down into its place. The mob slowly walked away one by one. I noticed my mother holding a blanket around a woman whom I did not know. My father was upset at everyone and everything. This mob could have beaten us all to death if they had had the chance, and gotten away with it. It was common for mobs to take "justice" into their own hands, their anger based merely on gossip, especially against "blasphemous" women.

My dad gestured to us to quickly go upstairs and was impatient with the woman in the blanket. He blamed her for the mob and endangering our lives. I wasn't sure what she had done to cause the commotion, but father began yelling when we got upstairs about her running around naked in the streets. It was indecent in Pakistan for a woman to be without a scarf covering her hair. Rather than showing concern, people wanted to attack her. The woman appeared to be mentally unstable. It almost cost her her life. I felt very bad for her. Why was she out in the middle of the night on her own in the first place? It was not the safest place to be for women or girls even during the day, with the constant harassment they received. The woman was still acting oddly. She was screaming from a chair in the balcony that my father had placed for her. He told her to stop screaming and not move, until she calmed down. I watched the lady as she sat there helplessly. My mother ended up taking her inside the living room and watching her for the rest of the night. It was a stressful night for everyone. I had

never witnessed a mob that close before. It was like a scene
from a Bollywood movie, full of dramatics.

In the morning, the family of the woman found out
where she was and arrived. They explained to us that she
was mentally ill and had had an episode before running off
naked and screaming. She had not been properly treated
for her illness and the current medication she was on was
not very helpful. The woman was very scared and angry at
everyone, especially my father, who was the last person yelling at her. Once she and her family had gone, everything
became calm again. We went on about our business and
never saw or heard from her again.

I began to grow restless at home. The boredom inspired an
idea. I thought how nice it would be to have my father build
the dollhouse that he had promised. The idea alone excited
me. One day I waited for him to get home so I could speak
to him about it. Dusk came and my mother was praying
in the living room. I was looking out the window for my
father. Once my mother was done praying, she put together
a steak shorwa, a soup, with naan. It smelt amazing. My
father arrived and came into the living room for dinner.
We gathered around the mat with a big bowl of shorwa
and cut-up naan. My father broke the pieces of naan into
smaller ones and put them in the shorwa. We all shared
from one bowl and ate with our hands as usual. I wasn't
good at eating with my hands, so my parents would take
turns to correct me when I was making a mess. We enjoyed

dinner peacefully together that night. I think we were all pretty tired and drained from the year that was now almost coming to an end.

When we were finished eating, we cleaned up. Abdullah assigned me the task of wiping the mat and washing the dishes. Ruby was responsible for picking up the dishes and taking them to the sink. Somehow Abdullah had tricked us into thinking this was fair, since he was the one supervising the work. He was getting away with a lot by guilt-tripping my parents. He enjoyed the benefits of being the first child and oldest, but also hated it because he was expected to be a leader. Life was too busy to keep track of his issues, so my parents continued to trust him. He had days of being good, but most of the time he took advantage and bossed us around. I became quieter as a person because of his bullying.

I had put off speaking to my father about my dream doll-house. I decided it was best to wait for a day when he was off work and free. One day I saw him in his comfortable house clothes, wearing a traditional outfit with long top and loose pants called perahan tunban. He had grown out his beard a bit more and looked much older. Later that morning I found him working on something on the roof. It was a bright, sunny, and hot day. I asked Ruby to come with me to see what father was doing. He looked very irritable and seemed to be cleaning up the small storage area. The roof was large and dusty with enough space to bike and run around. I looked around for the tricycle to keep busy, while watching out for a good opportunity to speak to him.

It was parked at the back corner of the roof and I ran up to it, Ruby following behind.

I was happily riding the bike around, laughing, and then Abdullah came up; he saw me enjoying myself and wanted to have a turn on the bike too. Then mother showed up on the roof too with her camera in hand. She began taking pictures of us with the bike. Abdullah stood behind me as I posed, laughing. Then we took a group photo of us sitting against the wall with the sun beaming down on us. We were all either squinting or had our hands up to block the sun. Once we had taken the picture, we headed back down the steps from the roof. I was the last one out before father locked up, and once he was done, I asked him if he could build a mini house rather than a dollhouse for us. He was in a happier mood and said "*azaar dafa*," a thousand times. I was thrilled to hear that. I had accomplished my mission successfully.

Waiting for my mini house made my days worthwhile. As the days passed, I knew I was getting closer to its revelation. I would daydream about it being pink, large, and full of dolls inside to play with. My father had made a promise to me. The weather was getting cooler as winter approached, and I became a bit worried about my mini house; I had not heard any updates from my father. I thought he wanted to surprise me and maybe that was why he never brought it up.

About a month after his promise, I finally decided it was a good time to ask him about it. I assumed he was building the house on the roof, so when I saw him leave the roof, I ran up to him before he locked the door. Ruby and her friend were running behind me playing and crowding the stairwell while he was trying to walk down. He was bothered by them and was telling them to get out of the way. "*Birain, birain,*" Leave, leave, he demanded angrily. But I was too excited about my mini house to realize that he was in a bad mood. "*Baba, khanaym jor kadayn?*" Daddy, did you build my house? I asked. "*Chi khana?*" What house? he asked. "*Guftain kay khana choocha maysauzain ba ma,*" You said you would make me a small house? I said, "*Chi? Khana? Ma khana namayzausum!*" What!? House? I'm not making a house! he angrily replied and shooed us away.

My perception of him as the only person on this Earth who would never break but only protect my heart was absolutely destroyed. The image I had of him as my father, the king, and I as one of his princesses, was instantly gone. It was tragic. He had handled me roughly as if I was some kind of rubbish, not his little girl. As if he had no heart and I had no heart either. I looked him right in the eye for not only breaking his promise but mistreating me. I never thought a father could ever break a promise or show no concern. I had looked up to him as being superhuman, someone who could do no wrong to me. What kind of father talks to his daughter like that? I asked myself. I did not feel special anymore. He made me feel like I was not worthy of love and respect. Even worse, that he was not a father to me anymore. He was not gentle or kind to me. I had forgiven and forgotten how he had punished Abdullah and Ruby once, but now he broke my heart. The damage was irreparable. I could never see him the same way again.

My father had been a light to me and now he caused me darkness. My world became less magical that day. The special bond between us was gone.

The distance between my father and me was only growing. I did not think of him as someone I could confide in or seek for help. I already had difficulty asking for help and that incident was a confirmation that it was pointless to do so. I was confident that I could not rely on him or anyone for that matter. The grown-ups in my life were troubled and distressed.

Winter arrived and we stayed indoors even more. Mother was preparing the home for our first visit from family overseas. Her brother Qairi was to arrive next morning from Canada. He was helping us with our immigration application. I had never met Maumau Qairi. ("Maumau" means maternal uncle.) Maumau Qairi was younger than my mother; he had fled to Iran with his two daughters before settling in Canada a few years later. They were my first cousins and I had never met them. I had many cousins around the world whom I probably would never meet because of the war in Afghanistan.

We were all doing our best to assist our mother in cleaning the home in preparation for Maumau's visit. Anytime we hosted anyone in our home, our mother would become extra stressed. I did not enjoy us hosting because it would turn into a day's worth of work. The day of any guest sharing dinner with us was one of nonstop chores with constant criticism about not doing things right. The best part was finally eating, but we had to wait for the guests to serve themselves first. Then we would wait till they were eating before we could even think about ourselves. Mother would push us to ask them if they needed anything or to insist they take more. Hospitality was very important in our culture.

Guests were seen and treated as royal visitors in your home. It was a serious duty and honor to host. A responsibility that our mother took very seriously. She became a manager commanding us to run the home like a luxury hotel and obsessed about customer satisfaction. Your guests must leave feeling better than they arrived!

I was dreading all this, but I was looking forward to meeting Maumau Qairi for the first time. I hoped he was kind and loving. I also wished that he would bring us some gifts and toys. After spending the day doing chores, we all went to bed exhausted.

Once I woke up, I went straight to the kitchen to see all the food we had prepared for the day, like stuffed beef dumplings called mantu, stuffed chive dumplings called aushak, chicken stew called qorma, and lola kebob—a fried, rolled ground beef kebob. There were certain Afghan foods which we made only for guests because they were time-consuming and expensive. The best recipes were reserved for maymaunees, *guest hostings*. Everything was still covered and in the balcony to cool overnight. I snuck into one of the plates and grabbed one lola kebob and sat there savouring its taste, thinking how much it felt like being home in Kabul again. I had become really sneaky when it came to food. I was always quick to grab something when my mother wasn't looking. I filled in the space left by the missing lola kebob and perfectly covered the whole tray back again.

When I emerged from the kitchen, I heard my parents laughing with someone outside our apartment. The front door was ajar and I peeked outside to see where the unrecognizable laughter was coming from. There stood in between my parents a man I had not seen before. He saw me instantly, my head poking out, and looked down with a smile. I came out and slowly walked to my mother's side, and hid behind the long brown scarf she had decided to wear that day. She explained which child I was and my uncle nodded his head. He looked very comfortable being in Islamabad. I wondered how far he must have travelled and the risk he took to return to this part of the world where I was becoming more scared and felt unsafe. Then my mother called out to Abdullah and Ruby. We all walked towards the end of the hall to take a photo together. Abdullah, Ruby, and I were placed in the front while my mother and her brother stood behind us.

I was quiet and very observant of Maumau Qairi. If we were to move to where he lived, it would mean spending a lot of time with him and his family. I was making sure that I liked him and what to expect living with him if we settled in Canada. We sat together for a breakfast feast. My father had baked fresh naan; he was also best at frying Afghan-style eggs with lots of tomatoes, garlic, and onions seasoned with salt and pepper. The smell was like nothing else. He would cook it at a perfect temperature and take it out in time before it was too fried or dry. We also had qaimak chai, which was a creamier version of sheer-chai. I hadn't had fried eggs in a while and was enjoying having our guest over.

When we were finished eating, my father stayed behind to speak with Maumau Qairi, and Ruby and I helped our mother clean up. My mother was very busy this morning again, rushing us to put things away quickly and start washing so she could reuse the cutlery and dishes. We spent most of the morning in the kitchen cleaning and preparing meals for later that day. There was an exciting energy to the day. There must be some great news for Maumau Qairi to have come all the way to visit us here. I was mentally prepared to move to another country. The possibility of moving to a better place also felt overwhelming for what it might mean for our future. I kept going back to the thoughts and questions about becoming further from myself and who I was—of possibly losing and forgetting my essence. I had to control this event to some degree, because it was a battle in my eyes. A battle between my homeland and native identity against a very foreign country and culture. There was this heavy feeling upon me as the reality sank in. My emotions were strong, things were changing fast, and I was losing track of my thoughts. I felt like I was losing control of my life again. I had that paralyzing feeling again of needing help or someone to confide in. I decided to focus on the task at hand to calm myself.

My father left with Maumau Qairi to give him a tour

of our neighbourhood and talk more about our application status for going to Canada. I did not know any details, only that somehow, with someone's approval, we would be let into that country. I had learned that you had to apply for permission to travel the world that we all shared freely. It was a scary reality, that you could not escape hell on Earth unless someone else allowed you to escape. I felt more and more trapped in Islamabad and never wanted to be this vulnerable or weak again. Why were we not free to leave as we pleased, especially when we had been in danger back in Kabul and were mistreated in Pakistan? Why couldn't we just fly out wherever was safer and better for us? I didn't understand the world. I wanted to return to Kabul some-day, but I also didn't want to be stuck in a war. There was no certainty about when Kabul would become peaceful again.

When they returned, it was dinner time. They had ended up touring and talking all day. Maumau Qairi came in explaining out aloud to my father that he would be stay-ing at a hotel and not to worry about him. We had already set up the things he would need to be comfortable sleeping in our living room, but that was not necessary anymore. He would stay for dinner and then head back to his hotel. I realized it would be a very short visit. My father was more relaxed and content since Maumau Qairi's arrival. My mother signaled for us to set up the dinner mat and plates as she prepared chai for them. She looked happy as well. There was a sense of hope building again.

We had aushak, mantu, lola kekob, chicken qorma,

cooked spinach, and Kabuli rice. Abdullah helped by preparing the salad, something he enjoyed and was good at. Kabuli salad was made with diced onions, tomatoes, cucumber, cilantro, lemon, and salt. There was also a bowl of yogurt mixed with mint as sauce for our meal. We had not had such a wonderful feast since the good times in Kabul when I was much smaller. Once Maumau Qairi and my father had filled their plates and started to eat, it was our turn to fill our plates. My mother was always last and would usually refuse to eat until everyone finished eating. She would eat on her own after we had put the plates away. She didn't like to eat in front of her guests. She thought it was shameful to join in because the feast should be prepared solely for her guests and she would ensure everyone had everything they needed. She would not sit down or stop moving around while they ate. There was always something to do or refill. Eventually, once the guests were comfortable and settled, she would join us.

I listened to my parents' conversation with Maumau as they discussed the good and bad memories of life in Kabul. I learned that my father had been wrongfully imprisoned when the government of the time was overthrown by a Soviet-backed coup. President Daoud Khan was assassinated, and his family murdered in the presidential palace. Daoud Khan had overthrown the monarchy, which was led by his own first cousin, King Zahir Shah. The communist government of the Peoples' Democratic Party of Afghanistan was led by Muhammad Taraki. He was president for the first year before being assassinated by his right-hand man, Hafizullah Amin, a highly educated man who had studied in America, with a master's degree in education. He ordered the imprisonment and execution of many innocent men. Thousands of mostly young men were executed and dumped in a mass grave behind the prison. My father could have been one of them if it were not for the delays due to the massive numbers of prisoners. He spoke about how the prison rooms were packed with no beds or bathrooms. They never left the barred rooms and if they needed to use the bathroom, it was in front of each other in a bucket. My father was speaking to my maumau quietly but I was interested and paid close attention. His story was unbelievably sad. It helped me to understand him better.

I was accustomed to hearing dark, heavy depressing conversations among grown-ups. There were a lot of bad news and stories to be shared and pondered upon from the past decade alone. Things had been getting only worse. Later they went on to talk about the extreme poverty in Kabul currently. The stories of people selling their children in exchange for food. One father was so distraught by the poverty and hunger, he threw himself from a mountain after telling his family that he could not bear to watch his children starve in front of him. There were stories about how the Taliban were casually executing and torturing people for fun. A distant relative who was living alone in the outskirts was dragged out of his house and sprayed with bullets in front of his home for no apparent reason. Men were taken from their homes, chained in torture rooms, and whipped daily till their backs were bleeding. They would take children up to the mountains for the foreign militant groups like Al Qaeda. These militants had been supported by America and used to combat the Soviet Union during the Cold War in a proxy war between the two military superpowers.

We survived but there were so many Afghans left behind, trapped in the living nightmares of war. I wish I had not heard these stories, and I could not enjoy my food anymore. I felt sad inside. I tried to tune out the conversation and enjoy my dinner. Their conversation continued and I distracted myself from paying attention. What could I do to help as a little girl? How could I save us? How could I save myself? How could I save my city? My country? My ancestry? Whoever was behind all this destruction was robbing us of everything that was ours. I felt helpless. Dinner came to an end and so did the dark night. I went to bed and cried myself to sleep over the images and sounds in my head. The old man crying for his starving children before jumping off a cliff. I would imagine his bloodshot eyes, his cries of despair. The helpless young man riddled with bullets fired in cold blood and at close range as if his life had no meaning or value, just because he was living in the wrong place at the wrong time in the world. These were the new pieces of hurt I collected in my already heavy heart.

I could not accept and let go of the past or what my country had become. There was no escape. Pain was the only constant that defined me and reminded me of my homeland. I was becoming comfortable with the feeling of pain. I thought if I lived in it then I would always be close to who I was and where I was from. I began to tell myself that I would return, yet knew that it was impossible. It hurt to know the truth but I kept the lie going. I came from pain and I would live in pain. The stories lived inside me. There was no escaping anymore, my country's bleeding spirit lived within me. I came from it. I could feel it.

Maumau Qairi visited our home one more time before leaving the same week. He had been busy with my father all week with our application requirements. He came to say goodbye before heading off with my father to the airport. My parents were looking hopeful that entire week. I tried to focus on the positivity of eventually moving and meeting him again in his new land to which he would introduce us. Weeks went by with no updates. Things were pretty much back to usual.

One day our parents quickly took my siblings and me a couple of blocks down from our apartment to the camera shop. They spoke to the shop owner. He had a camera facing a blank white board and a tall stool in front of it. I had never had a picture taken alone. I thought it was a bit silly but my parents were very serious and rushed to get them all done properly and immediately. When it was my turn, my father picked me up and sat me on the stool, which didn't feel very stable. I didn't take the photo shoot seriously and stuck my chin up at the camera like I was not one to mess around with. The photographer finished taking a photo of each of us, then we all headed quickly home. There was that rush of energy again that I had felt when Maumau Qairi had visited.

I could sense that something was about to change. My parents were preparing us for something but did not tell us what.

A few days later, everything changed.

My parents were running around the apartment putting things together to pack. My father pulled out all of the suitcases from our storage. Our parents had booklets with the photos that we had taken at the photo shop. My mother grabbed the booklets and put them safely in a briefcase. *"Arakat maykunaim sabah,"* We will be departing tomorrow, she told us, *"Tayara e mah myaya sabah,"* Our airplane flight is tomorrow. I had never been on an airplane or even to an airport. I had no idea what it was like but had seen it occasionally in the sky. I wasn't sure where we were headed either. My parents were too frantic getting us ready to have even a second to stop and explain. It was a long, hectic day of packing. My mother had all our outfits ready for our travel. She wanted us to wear our matching Mickey Mouse grey sweatsuits except for Laila, who was too small for one. Laila was almost a year old and was attempting to walk. She had no clue what was going on and looked quite entertained by all the movement around her.

My parents woke us up before the sun was out. They hurried us into our outfits and we were suddenly off to Islamabad International Airport in a cab. I was too sleepy to pay attention. Somehow we reached the airport and boarded the plane.

I drifted in and out of sleep throughout the whole flight from Islamabad to our layover in Holland called Schiphol Airport. There were a lot of white people everywhere. A white man came up to us and helped take our luggage away. My father told us that we would be staying overnight in Holland and so we took a cab to an apartment hotel. It was late at night, and I dozed off during the ride.

When we got to our hotel, the host walked us to our unit. He opened the door and I saw two big beds in one room for the first time. There was a lamp and bedside table for each bed. There was a phone in the room and a big mirror. Abdullah, Ruby, and I started exploring everything and giggling at the newness of it all. My father was busy figuring out how to get us food. We were all tired but more so hungry from the long flight from Pakistan. My parents looked happy but nervous. I probably hadn't seen them that nervous since we fled Afghanistan. Of course it wasn't the same kind of nervousness. They weren't nervous about our lives being at risk but by this very new beginning. I didn't know what was beginning but I knew our time in Pakistan had ended. It felt like we were far away from Pakistan now. This place was so different. Outside the hotel there were bright lights, clean, wide sidewalks, grass everywhere, and very modern buildings. It was also very quiet and not crowded.

Sometime later, my father brought us some food to eat. It wasn't a lot but it was enough to help us go to bed. My mother told us to go to sleep early because we had another flight the next day. I was very confused because where we landed was so nice. It was good enough for me to stay. I didn't understand why we were leaving this place too.

The next morning, we headed back to Schiphol Airport and jumped on to another flight. This airplane was much bigger, brighter, spacious, and nicer, plus it had meals right away with a little table you could pull down in front of you. There were so many different kinds of people, mostly white and older grown-ups. They were in Western clothing and made no eye contact.

Everything was so organized—even the way people gestured to each other. It was like everyone had their own personal space and their own personal bubble. It wasn't a talkative plane and the rest of the flight remained like that until Abdullah fell ill. He was throwing up and started shaking on the floor. The flight attendant rushed to help my father take him to a section where they laid him down. I had never seen Abdullah like that. I ran out of my seat to see what was happening. They emptied three seats and laid him on his side. He was having a seizure, but my parents had no clue what was wrong with him. My mother was moved to the front of the plane so she could sit near Abdullah while he recovered.

The old, white couple that I was sitting beside were reading newspapers. I stared at them, seeing how different they were. They spoke a different language, behaved very cautiously, and had nice clothes. The man wore an interesting-looking watch and glasses. He noticed me staring and offered a sealed snack he had left over in front of him. I smiled at my first interaction with these new people. It was all so interesting and different.

Toronto, Ontario

Winter 1995

I FELL ASLEEP AGAIN and woke up as we arrived at another airport, called Toronto Pearson International. After a long time we finally got our luggage finally and were directed to some kind of machine. Our luggage was rolling through it and someone was checking each suitcase. We had a lot of them of all sizes. We were a family of six that had taken everything we could with us. My father had even managed to bring our Afghan carpets. He said how proud he was that he could bring everything, but the airport person was complaining how heavy it all was. Once we were done with the luggage, we stepped out into an even brighter, larger place full of glass windows everywhere. There were so many lights, screens, people, and sounds. It was a busy day at this airport. I was scared I would get lost because my parents went back and forth using the telephone and trying to get help.

While we were sitting beside our luggage, my mother was ready to take a picture, even though we were exhausted after the two flights and what felt like many days of travelling. I stared into nowhere, Laila was on the floor, Abdullah was zoned out still from his seizure, and Ruby was staring all around. We were ready to finally arrive at a place with beds again. After we had waited almost an hour, Maumau Qairi showed up and took us out of the airport. I was very scared. I knew we were in Canada, our new home, but it felt like I had never really landed because my heart was still in Kabul. A piece of me was missing.

My father put all our luggage in the back of a very big car and then sat in the front seat, while the rest of us shoved and squeezed ourselves in the back. It was nighttime. The roads were wide with lights everywhere. The window was down a bit with a fresh but freezing air coming through. I was not very happy that my parents had not explained any of this to us. I looked around and everyone was just focused on our destination, which was wherever Maumau Qairi took us. I assumed it was to his house.

I repeated to myself that we had finally arrived in Canada. We were so far from Afghanistan. I looked behind to see through the back window as we drove off farther from the airport. Pearson Airport looked like a huge space-ship. I had never seen such a bright building before. I could see its whole shape. It looked even more impressive from afar. No one asked any questions, but I had a lot. My first question was if we were ever going to return to Kabul. I did not know if I wanted to be neutral or optimistic about our new life. I had this new obsession, to hold onto what I felt like I was leaving behind forever. I also felt further loss of control over my life and destiny. It was like holding on too tightly to a stem full of thorns. I was in love with the flower that was Kabul, but it was hurting me to hold on to it. I had to let Kabul go but I wasn't ready or knew how to.

I held on tight to the vision of returning to Kabul some day with my family. I held tight to the lie I told myself that this was just a vacation. I chose not to accept or embrace this new chapter. I let the thorns cut me like the bleeding garden that I was and always will be. I did not enjoy the ride to Maumau's house. There were so many unanswered questions with no one to ask. I sat quietly drowning in my thoughts and pain, making up stories of what we were doing here. I closed my eyes and fell asleep.

The next morning, I found myself in a large, very cold and dark room below the house. We were still sleeping on the *toshaks* spread around the corners of the room. My father must have carried me downstairs from the car. We were all beaten up from the long trip, physically and emotionally exhausted from all the changes in our lives in such a short period of time. We could never do this again. All we wanted was to be settled finally for good. No more running. No more fleeing. No more chasing. Just peace and stability from now on.

I started to imagine what was upstairs and what my extended family was like. The steps going up were old wooden planks. They didn't look very safe or fun to climb. One half of the basement was pitch black with a curtain covering it. That didn't feel very comfortable to be next to either. I wondered what was behind the curtain, probably storage but it looked scary to go past.

Slowly my family members began to wake up. My father was the first one after me and he went straight upstairs—I guessed he had already had a tour and knew where the bathroom was. My mother woke up after him. She noticed I was awake and told me to come upstairs with her. We slowly and quietly went up the stairs and opened the door into the main floor. It was a bit warmer and no one was around. I could hear my father in the washroom. There was a huge dining table with chairs. My mom pointed to a chair for me to sit and wait. She went into the kitchen and found a woman quietly cooking. It was probably her sister-in-law, Mari. They greeted each other and then waved at me. I was hesitant to approach or speak so I sat very still where I was. My mother brought me an apple to eat. My father was finished with the bathroom and I ran in next.

When I came out, my mother was helping Khala Mari with breakfast. I sat back down at the dining table and began to eat my apple. The house had an eerie feeling to it, with an uncomfortable silence. I felt myself becoming more quiet and hesitant as I sat there. There were no toys around or anything interesting in sight for a girl to play with. I could see the backyard from where I was sitting. The living room facing the kitchen had a large and wide window. It was snowing and there was a lot of snow on the ground already. I got out of my seat to look at it closely through the glass door. I had never seen so much snow before. It looked heavy as it fell. Khala Mari came out of the kitchen with my mother with some serving dishes to set on the table. There was a plate of naan and rote which is a dry, dense cake. I love rote. It tastes like home. Then my mother told me to head back downstairs. Walking back down the creaky wooden stairs, however, I awoke Abdullah and Ruby. They looked just as confused about where they were as I was before.

We had had the most hectic last few days and finally arrived at a very secluded basement that we were not expecting to be in. I must have been very optimistic when I thought we would spend our first night in this country in comfortable bedrooms, especially after such a rough journey. It felt like we were being hidden down here where there were no windows. I did not enjoy a minute of being down there. Mother took me towards the luggage and told me to pick out some day clothes to wear. I loved dresses but it was too cold to wear one in the basement or outdoors. I decided to wear black cotton pants with a dress over it and a black sweater. It was common to wear skirts and dresses over pants or under sweaters in Pakistan, which was very conservative. It wasn't safe for girls to show skin, dress feminine, or even look feminine, which is probably why my hair was cut above my ears. I decided to dress up as much as I could, since, despite the basement, today felt celebratory after arriving safely and spending our first night in Canada.

Once we were all dressed, mother asked us to stand against the curtain dividing the basement to take our picture. I was feeling good about my outfit. I posed smirking with my hand on my left hip. Ruby stood to the left of me and Abdullah was to the left of Ruby. We were all a bit scared and trying to make the best of the changes and the new beginning. Mother stayed behind to take care of Laila as the three of us started going upstairs for breakfast. It was very scary because we could hear our cousins, who were awake and talking to each other. We were shy and stared at each other for a moment behind the basement door. Abdullah looked behind him, his eyes wide open, hesitating to go first. He opened the door and we all cautiously made our way behind him. Abdullah went straight to our father, who was sitting on the living room couch, a big, dark brown leather one, and sat down beside him. Ruby and I followed. Khala Mari was still preparing breakfast and came to serve chai to my father. In the hallway our two cousins were chatting. They were tall, skinny girls with long, jet-black hair. They looked like Ruby, especially the one who looked older. She had hazel eyes, and the younger, shorter sister had bright blue eyes like her father, Maumau Qairi. They kept themselves busy with each other and did not come up to meet us. We felt uncomfortable and wondered if we should go up to them.

Ruby shoved me by the arm, whispering "*Buro*," Go, telling me to go and introduce myself first. I shoved back, "*Nay!*" No! I was not going to risk putting myself in an embarrassing or unwelcoming situation. I could read their energy and body language clearly. They did not appreciate us being there.

Maumau Qairi walked into the house with a couple of grocery bags in his hands. He looked red in the face from the cold. He had probably been shovelling all morning as well. It was nice to see a familiar face again, but he looked

stressed. His daughters helped him by grabbing the bags
and went into the kitchen to their mom. I knew something
was not right and we were going to be here briefly. No one
looked genuinely happy, but they all did what they needed
to do. Ruby and I began to look out the window behind
us. We passed the time watching the snow fall and talking
about what we noticed outside. There were many dark
brown attached houses around. The leaves were all pretty
much gone from the trees. There wasn't anyone outside
playing. The neighbourhood was quiet and nothing like
Islamabad, where there were always crowds of people outside. It was just a lot of attached houses and no stores or
parks in sight. Then a group of teenagers walked by with
their hoods on.

Mother came upstairs with Laila and put her down.
Laila was a pleasant infant now who didn't need much to
keep her busy. She was very observant and quiet. She grav-
itated towards me when my mother left her side. She also
wore a dress over her pants, and a sweater. I was starting
to get hungry and bored just staring out the window, when
finally my mother went into the kitchen and came out with
serving plates. They had run out of milk and eggs, which
caused us to wait a bit. There were fried eggs, boiled eggs,
chicken liver, apricot jam, cream cheese, and qaimak chai.
I started to relax a bit and enjoyed the generous breakfast.

While we were all sitting and eating, our two cousins
joined us. They were still not very friendly or approachable
and kept to themselves. I didn't pay them any mind, but
it was not helping the already uncomfortable mood of the

home. The grown-ups were talking. I also lost interest in hearing all the things we needed to do, now that we had arrived. It felt overwhelming starting back at the bottom again. I tried to stay positive and enjoy the moment, I just wanted to be a kid again—carefree and playing. I still did not have any toys.

After breakfast, my mother and Khala Mari were busy cleaning up together. Maumau Qairi invited us on a tour of the house. I was thrilled because I wanted to see my cousins' bedrooms and their toys. I looked forward to playing with them. At the front of the first floor was the main living room. The lights were off and there were three white antique-style sofas that looked very uncomfortable. We finally headed towards the second floor. The stairs were carpeted and much nicer. There were four bedrooms—two on each side with a big washroom in the middle that had a standing shower like ours in Islamabad. We quickly peeked into Maumau Qairi's room—it was beautiful, with a wide bed in the centre and matching tables and a dresser. The mahogany bed had wooden poles at each corner. It looked very royal. I had never seen such a beautiful bedroom or that kind of furniture before. There was a smaller room next to his which was an office for his business. Looking at the posters and banners in the room, it looked like he owned some trucks.

Then we got to the bedrooms across, which belonged to my two cousins. The first room on the right had a similar bed with poles, but this one was white with transparent white curtains tied at each corner. It was a bed designed for a princess. Maumau Qairi said it was his eldest daughter Soraya's room. It also had a white dresser with a beautifully shaped mirror above it. It was an absolutely beautiful girl's bedroom, and the bed seemed a dream to sleep in. I wanted it badly. The next bedroom was exactly the same. It was the second daughter Sitara's room. And she actually had stuffed animals seated neatly one by one on her bed against the wall. I ran inside and looked at them closely. They were very cute but not dolls. I couldn't believe she had so many of them. She was the luckiest girl in my eyes to have such a bedroom. I never had a toy, let alone an elegant bedroom all to myself. But I was optimistic about the future, knowing that this was possible.

Soraya and Sitara came up the stairs running. Sitara saw me staring at the stuffed animals and said in our language that she was sorry that I could not play with them because she had them in a certain order and for display purposes only. Then she pointed towards her dresser to bring my attention to her pictures of herself. She looked like she loved fashion and makeup. I acknowledged by saying they were really good. I didn't feel very comfortable to say anymore or stay in her room any longer. I slowly made my way out, disappointed that she wouldn't let me touch her stuffed animals. It was not a good first impression. I could overhear her saying to Maumau Qairi that she hated kids especially in her clean room.

My father called my name to head back down. Abdullah and Ruby had already left the house tour, which they found boring. We followed Maumau Qairi to the basement. He was explaining that there was an extra TV here that we could use to keep the kids busy. I was surprised to hear this because I did not notice a TV, but then again it was very dim in the basement, with one light bulb hanging from the ceiling. I was happy to hear this. There could possibly be new cartoons and channels that I'd never seen before. We walked to the back of the basement. In the far right corner was a tall brown TV stand with a cover over it. Maumau Qairi pulled off the cover. The TV was probably four times bigger than ours in Islamabad. He started looking for something. It was a remote control with a bunch of buttons. This TV was very advanced and I knew I was going to be hooked to it. Suddenly it turned on and the picture was clear and in colour, with no static! Abdullah and Ruby heard the TV and came downstairs. Maumau Qairi said that his daughters played video games here and he pointed to a grey device beside the TV. I had never played video games before but was curious to learn. Then he showed me how to change the channels by simply pushing the buttons. Abdullah and Ruby were impatiently waiting for their turn to play with the remote. I handed it over to Abdullah to choose something since there were so many channels. My father and Maumau Qairi walked away, continuing their discussion about our living situation. I didn't know how long we would stay in that house but it seemed a little bit more bearable with this TV distracting us and helping the time fly. Everything was in English so we spent most of the time guessing what was going on.

We spent the rest of the day in the cold basement watching TV. We used our blankets to stay comfortable. Soraya and Sitara kept to themselves, so we did not get to know them more. Abdullah was not offended by this, since he was a boy and it wasn't appropriate for male and female cousins to be close with each other. It was a very formal and distant relationship you would have with the opposite sex. The grown-ups would watch to make sure they weren't being too friendly. It was common in our culture for cousins to marry, even first cousins, since it was better to marry those within your village with whom you grew up. However, Ruby and I were bothered and hurt by the cousins' lack of interest in us. We were younger than them. Still, we thought they should care enough to show us some concern and kindness in this new country. They were our cousins.

It wasn't even a week before my mother started packing our things again. She looked disappointed and worried. "*Bayat beraim,*" We have to go, she said. She didn't say anything else and probably didn't know the details of where we were suddenly off to next. We hurried to get ourselves ready to leave. We packed up everything and helped to take it upstairs. It was obvious now that we were not coming back. We left nothing behind. My father hurried us out into a cab without properly saying goodbye to the family, obviously unhappy at what felt like being kicked out. It seemed very unfair, and we kids didn't have a clue what had happened. In our culture relatives looked after each other. Maumau was my mother's brother.

And so in the middle of a rough and heavy winter, we

were off to another place to live. I just hoped that it was warmer and more welcoming.

It was my first time seeing this new city during the day. We had been indoors during our first few days here and had arrived at night so we had not seen much. Everything looked perfect in the way the city was designed. The air was brighter, cleaner, and fresher. The roads were smooth, clean, and wide. Then at a distance from where we were driving, I saw tall building towers for the first time. We began to get closer and closer to them until we were driving right next to them. This part of the city was much busier, crowded, and full of stores. It reminded me more of Islamabad. Crowds of people and very little space in between buildings. However, the store windows here were large with mannequins perfectly placed. All the stores had open doors through which people could go freely inside, whereas in Islamabad there were wide open entrances with metal gates you pulled to close at night. The store clerks or owners would be sitting at the entrance waiting to help a customer. Things were very different here. I could see through the windows how spacious everything was. There were also lots of beautiful decorations. Many trees had lights on them. I assumed it was a holiday. I enjoyed the ride into this busy part of the city.

Finally we arrived at our destination. I did not know exactly where we were. From the worried looks on my parents' faces, I guessed that wherever we had arrived was not by their choice. Moving to this country was a lot more difficult than we thought. We were so far away from home.

We were able to have our own apartment in Pakistan, even with its discriminatory rent. I think my parents must have spent everything they had to get us here because we ended up having to stay in someone else's home. The cab parked in front of a huge brown building with a triangle roof and a cross in front of it. It looked like a religious place from the praying hands on the sign outside. The entrance was through a large brown double door. Once all of our luggage was taken out, my father was buzzing about trying to get hold of someone. I stared around me and saw a lot of people walking by fast, minding their business. No one was interested in who we were. I remember in Islamabad how more sociable it was, everyone comfortably stared at us when we arrived, asked questions, or introduced themselves. People were very interested in any change in their community. This city was so big that no one batted an eyelid at seeing us. Just like on our airplane flight, people paid no attention to anyone around them. The world had become very big just standing in the midst of these towers.

After a few rings, a lady popped her head out of the door. She looked at us to figure out who we could be. Maumau Qairi and his wife had come with us, so he was able to explain to the lady who we were and why we were there. The lady opened the door wider and waved for us all to come inside. It was the tallest room that I had ever been inside. It was very dim with natural lighting mostly, but I could see that there were countless benches and a stage in front. We walked into a brighter hallway that led to some steps going up. The second floor had a long hallway with many doors leading into rooms. The first room was an office, which we entered behind the lady. It had a large glass window and a small lit tree. We sat wherever we could. I didn't understand what the adults were saying but it looked like we were going to be left here. I spent the time playing with the tree, while Maumau Qairi helped my parents to fill out some papers. After what felt like a long time, the lady asked us to follow her out into the hallway. We passed many closed doors and then there was one room that was half open. We passed it and stopped in front of a closed door to which the lady had a key. She unlocked it and gave the key to my father. She opened the door wide and held it for us. The room had one window with six beds. Two of them were bunk beds. We were a family of six so I knew this must be where we were now staying. I did not like it at all, it was nothing like our apartment. All of us were in one single room with only beds. It was another rough beginning for us. I realized that we were in a shelter for refugee families. I was surprised and felt hurt that my uncle had been so quick to drop us off here.

The lady then gave us a tour of the rest of the floor. There was an open kitchen for everyone to use. There was also a room full of many showers for women and children to share. Around the corner was a storage room. There were a bunch of boxes and cans of food on shelves as well as some boxes of clothes. I started to slowly explore the storage room. I dug into one of the boxes and to my happy surprise found a stuffed doll. She was a tall doll with red hair split in two ponytails made of yarn. She was soft like a pillow that you could squeeze and hug. I grabbed it right away and began playing with it. The lady then quickly got a call on her phone, and we had to leave. I held on to the doll and asked my mother if she would let me keep it. The lady looked at my mother who was rushing out and nodded her head to say yes. I was overjoyed to have my first doll ever, and she was so big and cozy. I was in love. I had been dreaming about this moment forever and it finally came true. I walked along the hall proudly holding my doll against my chest. I was very protective of her. I wanted to take care of her and keep her as long as possible. She had a friendly smile, and I knew it was made with love and care. This was probably the happiest day of my life as a little girl. It made up for the broken promise of the dollhouse. I didn't care about it anymore. I was content with this doll now.

My father left with Maumau Qairi to get the rest of our luggage. My mother and Mari were privately speaking about the situation. I couldn't hear them fully, but it looked like my mother was being reassured that everything was good and going to get better. My mother had spent most of her life taken care of, never did she imagine she would be raising her children in a shelter in another country so far and different from her homeland. It was a lot to process that day.

However, my doll kept me positive. This country had gifted me a doll; I was very grateful and looking forward to collecting more dolls. I decided to name her Sara. Sara was my first best friend.

While my parents settled our stuff in the room, I sat on my bed playing with Sara. I chose the bed on the top right side by the window. We spent most of that morning in our room sorting our things. When lunchtime came, we followed our parents to a cafeteria. It was my first time trying the food of this country. It was two slices of cold white bread—nothing like naan. Naan was warm, thick, soft, and savory. In between this white bread was peanut butter and strawberry jam. It tasted bland but I was hungry at that point and finished my sandwich. While my parents were talking at the table, Ruby and I decided to explore. We went back into the hallway and found the kitchen. We began to look for better snacks and food. Unfortunately, the cupboards were mostly empty except for boxes of tea bags and sugar. Disappointed, we went back to the cafeteria. A lady began talking and brought out a TV. She invited the children to come forward and watch a Disney movie called *Beauty and the Beast*. She held up the VHS tape sleeve to show us the picture on it; it was of a beautiful girl wearing a golden gown. She was a brunette like me. I was thrilled to watch my first movie here. So far, the first day here was going good, even if we were all crammed inside one bedroom. The people here were trying to help us.

A few days went by in the shelter. One morning my mother told us we would be going to school that day. She helped us get dressed and we walked to a school nearby. It was very cold but I had on all of the winter clothing I needed, which the shelter had given us. The school was big with many classrooms. We walked down a long hallway.

We could hear our shoes echoing. A lady grabbed my hand and took me away from my mother and siblings. She pulled me into a red-carpeted classroom with many children running around and playing. I had to take off my winter boots and walk in with my unmatched big socks, one of which had a hole in it. I spent most of the time concentrating on keeping the hole part closed. The children were very busy and didn't notice me coming in. I was in the room with many strangers. I quietly made my way to the centre of the room where there was a big, brown rocking chair. I sat beside it trying to hide myself until someone could tell me what I was supposed to be doing. A bunch of kids came up towards the chair and began running around it. I decided it was better to sit on it. The kids were having fun all around me. My time in the classroom suddenly got cut short, when the lady who had dropped me off came in quickly and straight to me. She held up my head and searched through my hair, looking concerned. I didn't understand what she was looking for, but it felt humiliating. She grabbed my hand and rushed me out of the classroom.

Abdullah, Ruby, and I waited in the office confused and silent. My mother came to pick us up. It was a failure of a first day at school. I did not want to go back to that classroom after what had happened. How could I show my face after that? Everyone probably thought I was dirty and dangerous. My mother took us into our room and began to trim our hair even shorter than it already was. She went through my hair just like the lady at the school had and explained to me that we could not go back until our hair was cleaner. The school was upset about something called lice in our hair, which could spread to other children. We ended up spending the rest of the week at the shelter. None of us were looking forward to going back to that school and hoped that we would move out of here soon.

Weeks went by, during which my father began feeling aches in his head. After he had been to the hospital a couple of times, he was told that he needed an emergency brain surgery. We couldn't afford medical treatment in Islamabad, so when he finally got checked at the hospital here, they found that he was seriously sick. In order for him to recover safely, we had to move out of the shelter immediately. With the help of the hospital, we found an apartment that my parents could afford. We were suddenly moving again and had to pack our things, but without our father for the first time. We would have to wait until he was released from the hospital. At the end of the week we arrived at a very tall cream-coloured building. I brought my Sara doll with me and it made the experience easier. Inside the building lobby were two elevators that went up twenty-two floors. It was the tallest building I had ever been in. We got off on the eleventh floor and made our way to the end of the hall to door number 1111. My mother unlocked it with the key that the shelter had provided us.

The apartment was even bigger and brighter than the one we had in Islamabad. The living room was right in the centre, connecting to the kitchen and the bedrooms and washroom. Once we took our shoes off, we ran to choose our rooms. There were only three, so Ruby and I had to share one. We chose the smallest bedroom at the end of the hall on the left, facing my parents' room. There was also a balcony with the greatest view facing the CN Tower. We had no furniture, but we dragged our luggage to our rooms to put away our clothes in the closets.

Our kitchen had a big white refrigerator, but there was nothing in it yet. My mother let us know that the shelter would bring the rest of our stuff later that day. We needed our carpets at least to sleep on until we had furniture.

Finally, when the rest of our luggage was dropped off, we were able to set up our sleeping areas. Abdullah helped mother roll out all the carpets in the rooms. My parents had brought along four large heavy Afghan carpets from Islamabad. They were beautifully hand-made. Our home was slowly coming together. We then found a box of food that the shelter had packed for us. My mother grabbed a bag of rice and some cans to cook us a meal. She ended up baking rice with lubyah, fried red kidney beans cooked in tomato paste. I went back to my room to play with Sara. She was the light of my life who had truly made the last few weeks enjoyable. I took her everywhere with me and never felt alone because of her. Owning such a loveable doll made me feel confident.

The next day, mother took us out to discover what was within walking distance. We passed by a park and a basketball court in front of our building. Then we walked through a residential neighbourhood with houses. We discovered a bigger park after that. She let us stop to play for a few minutes and run around. Then we hurried off across the street where there was a supermarket. We went into as many stores as we could that morning to learn more about what was available. There were a grocery store, some offices, restaurants, and a bank. My mother went into the bank and had us wait while she spoke to them for more information. She knew some English from her university days. She was an ambitious and intelligent woman, and I knew she was going to get us settled well. It took a long while for her to finish at the bank, but once she was done, she came out with three children's booklets for us. She handed each of us a booklet of our own with our name on it and our first deposit. We had our own bank accounts for the first time ever. My booklet had a cute illustration of a white bunny on it with a pink background. I was very proud to own it.

Mother explained that she would try to do this as often as possible to build us our savings. Then she tucked them away in her purse for safety. I was very impressed by my mother for introducing us to saving money so young. It opened my mind to wanting more for myself in the future when I would be ready to take on more responsibility. After the bank, we went to a family doctor's office.

My mother found a Chinese doctor called Dr Lee. He was the only family doctor available, so we sat and waited for mother to register us there too.

While we were waiting, Ruby had gotten very hungry and tired. She was standing by a plant when she started to sway oddly before collapsing. All the grown-ups around rushed to pick her up and get her some water. We had been struggling nonstop for the past month in this new country, and my parents were losing track of our needs. The secretary gave us all a cup of water and we sat slowly drinking. I was hoping I wouldn't faint too because I didn't remember having breakfast either. We walked back home and had leftovers from yesterday. We had had a good day except for Ruby fainting and father still away from home.

A few days later, father came home from the hospital. He had a bandage still on his head and felt sore. He moved around slowly. But he made jokes about how he had survived a major operation and was proud of it. We let him rest in his room and mother took care of him until his stitches were fully healed. Once we were settled, with a big brown couch and beds for us all, my mother was able to focus on registering us at school. My father was the one who dropped us off on our first day. He walked me up to my classroom, which was much calmer than the one in the other school. A very old, tall white lady gently bent down to me and said hello. She had white hair and a sweet, warm smile. Her name was Ms Peace. She was my first real school teacher and I felt lucky to have her. She held my hand as my father walked away. I would not enter the classroom until I saw my father exit the school door with a last wave goodbye.

I was scared but Ms Peace was very kind. She walked me in and sat me down on the carpet before calling the class to sit down as well in front of her rocking chair. She introduced me to the class and held me by her side. I felt loved by her and safe in the school. Then she began reading a book that I didn't understand but enjoyed hearing. She walked over to a brown piano to the left of us and sat in front it. She began playing and singing some children's songs that I didn't know. And so my first day was amazing even though I didn't make any friends or speak to anyone. My classmates were kind to me and tried to introduce themselves one by one as I played quietly and alone. There were so many toys to play with that I didn't mind playing alone.

Once snack time came, everyone sat around in a circle. I didn't understand what was going on. I didn't have a snack bag like everyone else. Ms Peace came up to me with some cheese and crackers in a napkin when she noticed that I wasn't prepared. I looked around and saw everyone enjoying their snacks from home. I was ashamed of the snack Ms Peace had given me, because I felt poor eating it in front of the other kids who had brought their own, so I left the circle and sat behind the bookshelf pretending to read. Ms Peace came up to check on me.

My father came in the afternoon to pick me up. I was happy to see him, having made it through my first day without being rushed out of the classroom like previously. Ms Peace explained to my father that I needed to bring my own snack and showed him a snack bag as an example. I kept my head down while they finished speaking. Ms Peace was not aware that we were refugees who had come to the country with very little money and that my parents were very busy looking for jobs. My parents got us metal snack bags a few days later that you could open up like a brief-case. I loved my snack bag but my parents were too busy in the mornings to put anything in it. I didn't use my snack bag until one day when coming home from school I saw a toddler throwing unopened chocolate bars from the bal-cony. When his mother noticed, the toddler stopped and his mother apologized, but all the kids there grabbed them to keep, including myself. I managed to catch two chocolate bars. I saved them to take for my snack the next day. I was very proud to have a snack and use my snack bag for the first time. When snack time arrived the next day, I opened my snack bag slowly but was very shy. The other students had vegetables, fruits, bread, and drinks they openly placed in front of them. I did not want them to laugh at my snack because it was just chocolate, which wasn't very healthy. I decided to hide my snack and eat it privately by breaking it open inside my bag. I did not want to bring or use my snack bag ever again after that. I would just take a bite of the crackers that Ms Peace gave me when I didn't have a snack.

One day Ms Peace called me and another girl up to her. I had no idea what the reason was. She then started con-gratulating us for our birthday. I did not know it was my birthday and had never had a birthday party. She started singing the birthday song with the class. Once they were done, she asked the girl closest to her to show us what she got for her birthday. The girl was ready with two boxes in her hand, a doll inside each one. Ms Peace then asked me what I got for my birthday. I shook my head and showed her my empty hands. Ms Peace looked surprised and sad to realize that I did not know it was my birthday and had me standing up there without a gift to show or talk about. I think she felt disappointed in herself for putting me on the spot without confirming if I would have a birthday party. Most of the students were well-off and lived in the houses around the school.

The next day when school was ending, Ms Peace came up to me with a white container. She bent down and opened it slowly just for me to see. Inside was the most beautiful cupcake; it was also the first cupcake I had ever had. It was a vanilla cake with sky blue icing on top and sprinkles over it. Plus, she left a white candle stuck in the middle. She smiled and told me not to show it to the other students and to eat it only when I got home. On my way home, I ate my cupcake with so much joy. It was the best dessert I had ever had in a very long time. I couldn't remember when I had a cake last. Ms Peace was doing her best to make my first year in school positive. She was the best teacher I could wish for.

Unfortunately, Abdullah and Ruby weren't having as good an experience. Abdullah made friends quickly, but he was very behind academically. My mother was very upset when she found out that they would keep him back a grade. She started crying in front of us when she found out. She took it as a personal failure. Ruby was also not doing well, they put her in a smaller classroom for students with special needs. Because of this, she had trouble making friends. The other students treated those in the special class as different, they were teased and left out from everything. Ruby began blaming me for this at home because I had made my own friends and did not play with her. She was older than me, so my friends did not know her or want to play with her. It didn't help that Ruby was obviously not communicating or behaving normally. She would have tantrums, start acting hysterical, and become aggressive. I did not feel safe around her, since she would get violent with me. I had scratches on my arms for proof. Recess was a very confusing time for me trying to avoid her, as well as feeling sorry that she was alone and hiding from the embarrassment of having no friends. I felt guilty in my happy moments.

A couple of months passed, and spring was here—and so were the bugs! I loved bugs. They were my favourite things to play with during recess. I would find myself going in the far corners of the school field looking for them, especially caterpillars and grasshoppers. They were the most gentle and beautiful things on the earth for me. I loved them more than flowers or toys. The joy of holding a caterpillar or catching a grasshopper was enormous. The softness of the caterpillar crawling on my fingers and the beauty of a grasshopper staring up at me from inside my hands was amazing. Grasshoppers were very fast, so to catch one was a reward in itself. I also loved to observe ants on their ant hills. I would save worms when they were stuck on the concrete and at risk of being stepped on. "We have to save the worms!" I would shout on a rainy day and then gather anyone around me to help me put them back in the grass. I had stepped on a snail before and the crunching sound broke my heart. I raised my foot and saw the shell in pieces stuck under it.

The days became warmer and the bugs and flowers were born again. The lunch bell rang, and I ran outside with my two new friends—Amanda and Amina. They were both Black girls but from different parts of the world. Amanda was from Jamaica and Amina was from Somalia. I remember the first time I met them; I was intrigued by our differences. Their hair was not like mine and they would both style it with beautiful coloured hair clips. Their skin was darker but had a shiny glow and looked extra smooth. They were intrigued by me too and would play with my hair and say how shiny, straight, and silky it was. Amanda was very stylish and had the best matching outfits. She was a big fan of Tweety Bird, the cute yellow cartoon character.

Amanda had many clothes and accessories with Tweety Bird on them. I could tell her parents were well-off and she was better taken care of than Amina and me. I had never seen Black girls before until I met them at school in Toronto and they had never met an Afghan girl before me. We admired our differences and hung closely as a trio of friends.

We got to perform as a trio in our school play once, singing briefly, "Extra, extra, read all about it!" I remember the lights turning on us as we performed a little sassy dance across the stage before singing our lines and holding a newspaper. We also had a silly friendship song which I wrote, and we would dance to it during recess. It went something like "Friends! Friends! Friends forever! Did you ever know? Whoa!" We would laugh at ourselves at the end, but it was fun and got us dancing. We would pretend to be a trio music group practicing our song and then performing it for others during recess. We also had a secret hideout in the field where we had cleared out a bush to hang out inside like a hut.

One bright, warm spring day, the lunch bell rang loudly. Amanda, Amina, and I ran quickly together like we were one entity bursting through the playground doors. We raced towards the metal slide which was wide enough to fit all three of us. We held hands and slid down together, laughing hysterically. We were overjoyed by the early summerlike weather. Although normally I was very shy, something would come over me and I became the biggest daredevil of the trio when it came to recess shenanigans. The playground was large and full of adventure. I would run towards the highest pole, crawl up and hang down from my legs, my body swinging, a big smile on my face. I couldn't even tell how I learned to do this. The pole was some eight feet high. Amanda and Amina looked at me like I was crazy, but I loved the thrill and enjoyed impressing others. Luckily, the lunch monitors did not notice me, or they would have called me to put my nose against the wall for dangerous behaviour. "Come down Nila!" Amanda would shout. "Nila! You're scaring me!" Amina would say.

Sometimes we would go around the field to just walk and talk. One day I saw Ruby approaching us. Nothing scared me more than my two siblings. There was always something for them to fight about. "Nila!" Ruby called out my name and ran towards me. I looked at Amanda and Amina, who knew Ruby and did not like her. They had previous bad experiences with Ruby having outbursts when playing with them. "I don't want to play with your sister," said Amina, "I am going if she stays." "Ya! I do not want to play with her either. Nila, she is so strange," Amanda agreed. I tried to ignore Ruby and began to slowly walk away. But when Ruby caught up with us, she yelled, "Why are you walking away? I am calling your name!" I said, "I don't want to play with you." It was hard to say but I had no other choice. Amanda did not make the situation easier, saying, "Nila, if you play with her then I am leaving." I was clearly in the middle between my friends and my family.

"Are you going to listen to them, Nila? What kind of sister are you! You're choosing them over me!" shouted Ruby. The other kids in the field noticed the quarrel. "Why don't you play with your sister? That's mean," said some girl. "Ya, you're not even going to defend your sister," said another girl. No one knew what I was going through at home with Ruby, and why I was rightfully distant from her—I was trying to keep myself safe and sane. "You are a bad sister. You're choosing your friends over your sister," repeated Ruby. "I HATE YOU! DIE, NILA!" she screamed and walked away. The situation got the best of me and I screamed back, "You're a dog! I hate you!" I turned away and walked back to be with Amanda and Amina.

The school day came to an end and I waited outside near the playground watching the trail that my father took to come and fetch us. I was not in the mood to do anything but to stay still and avoid Ruby. I spotted my father coming on the trail and began to walk towards him. Once I reached him, he asked me where my siblings were. I walked with my father back to the school to look for them. We found Abdullah busy talking with his friends upstairs, and Ruby was still in class. Once we got Abdullah, we approached Ruby's class. The teacher was inside watching Ruby slowly getting ready. The teacher came up to us and spoke to my father very quietly so Ruby would not hear. She told him that Ruby was having a hard time still making friends and was very angry about it today. She said she found Ruby again hiding alone under the stairwell during lunch break. My father looked at me disappointed and confused. "*Shuma meefaume ke Ruby tanah asta?*" Do you know that Ruby is alone? he asked. I looked up at him with guilty eyes not knowing how to explain myself. "*Chura amrauyish sauteree namaykunee?*" Why don't you play with her?

The guilt inside me grew. I imagined Ruby in the darkness of a stairwell ashamed of having no one wanting to play with her. "*Aysh kas namahauya sauteree kuna amrauyish. Auzaur mayta kulagee,*" Nobody wants to play with her. She bothers everyone, I admitted. My father was ready to go and was fed up with us. Ruby saw me at the door and looked at me with disgust. "I hate her!" she said as she walked past me. Abdullah was still talking with his friends while waiting for us to be done with the teacher. He did not care about what was going on.

We walked home with our father. Ruby wouldn't let go

of her anger. She kept turning around to insult me. "You're a dog!" Ruby said. "No, you're a dog!" I shouted back. My father had to keep telling us to stop and be quiet. We picked up Laila from the preschool daycare located in our building's main floor. When we got home, things only got worse. Now I was trapped in a small apartment with Ruby. She continued to scream and yell at me at every opportunity. It did not help that I shared a bedroom with her. I made myself cereal for dinner and went straight to bed to end the miserable day.

Our first school year was coming to an end and the academic situation with both Abdullah and Ruby had not got better. Ruby was undergoing various professional examinations, which drained my parents with endless depressing news and medical appointments. Abdullah and Ruby would both not graduate from their grades, which brought on a scary cry from my mother at the back of the school parking lot. My parents had no idea how to support them and very little understanding of what their issues were. My father was failing to find or keep a decent job, so he was often depressed and his temper was worsening. He was home a lot of the time. My mother had found an office job and was providing for the family. We were struggling in poverty. We had not seen Maumau Qairi since he dropped us off at the Centre. I never learned what had happened between our families that week we stayed with them. My parents were now living separate lives since my mother would come home when we were all asleep. This only worsened my father's moods.

Summer break was almost near, and I was terrified.

SUMMER BREAK HAD STARTED. I made a new friend on my building floor named Agatha. She was chubby, with orange, short hair and white skin. She lived two doors down the hall on the opposite side. Her mother was a bit of a messy lady who was built quite big for her height. I didn't enjoy playing inside her apartment because it was quite dark with thick curtains, and it had a strange smell. One day we decided to play indoors in my bedroom with a boardgame that she brought over. We usually played with her toys because she had a lot to choose from. My bedroom door was shut and we were focused on the game.

"Do you hear that?" Agatha suddenly asked with concern. "Hear what?" I asked. "It's coming from the hallway. It sounds like your sister Ruby." For some reason, my hearing wasn't good or maybe Agatha had better hearing than me. I decided to get up and open the door. As I opened it, the sounds became louder. I looked back at Agatha and she followed me along to see where the sound was coming from. We walked into the hallway slowly and didn't see anyone. All the other doors were open except the bathroom door. Agatha pointed to the bathroom and tapped me on the shoulder. I opened the door and there was Ruby on the floor bent down with her back open and very red. She was crying and my father was slapping her over and over again with his hands. My mouth dropped and my eyes widened in shock at witnessing this physical abuse with Agatha behind me.

My father looked like he had lost his senses and was raging like a beast over Ruby. Agatha and I ran to the front door. I knew she wanted to get away and so I opened the door for her and quickly said bye. She did not want to risk getting into trouble with my father or being involved with what was going on. I ran back to the bathroom shouting to my father. "*Nako! Nako!*" Don't! Don't! I was in tears. I kept trying to pull his hands away from Ruby, who was helplessly crying. I felt powerless. I tried to pull her away from him. He started insulting her and began to yell about her using too much toilet paper. Ruby had a habit of clogging the toilet by playing with the toilet paper. We had only one washroom for a family of six so my father probably was fed up with the stress of the only toilet being broken again. However, his punishment was wrong and his temper uncontrollable. I was terrified seeing the beating and felt unable to save my sister.

Once I got myself into the washroom and had pulled Ruby away from him, he stopped and watched us leave. Ruby was absolutely red in the face and eyes. I knew she had been at fault, but she did not deserve that beating. She did not have a proper understanding of how to use basic things. We hid in our bedroom the rest of the day with our backs against the door, the lights off and in absolute silence.

We had no one to call or ask for help anyway, so we survived the day and never spoke about it.

Father was becoming worse, not better at home that summer. He was always angry about something and losing his temper. Mother was nowhere to be found during the day. By the time we awoke, she was gone, with no idea of what we were left to deal with—or maybe she had given up on the situation. How could she have not known how unsuitable he was to be watching us over the summer? Abdullah found himself busy outdoors most of the day since he was old enough to play on his own. He had a best friend who lived in the building across, where he spent most of his summer days. He had somewhere to escape to, but Ruby and I were stuck at home with father.

I became more protective of Ruby after what happened. I understood that she was extremely vulnerable, upsetting my father and risking punishment. I told her to stay away from him and to stop doing anything that angered him. But Ruby was limited in her understanding, so I knew it was bound to happen again. I prepared myself. I looked in our phone book to find numbers to call if it were to happen again. I found the number for the police and my mother's friend who lived in our building. My father was not going to get away with it next time, I thought. I will stop and expose him—I will show him how smart I am! I had nothing but anger against him now.

A few days passed and I decided to attempt to live normally again after the frightening incident. I walked with Ruby over to Agatha's apartment to see if she wanted to play. I knocked on her door. Agatha opened the door. She was clearly alone at home again. I asked her if she wanted to play with us, but she had the same scared face as the last time I saw her. "I can't. My mom said I can't come over anymore." I was hurt but understood. I was upset at my father for ruining my only friendship in the building. I nodded my head and said bye. We turned back to our apartment and decided to watch TV. Since father was not supervising us, we ended up watching whatever we wanted. There were mostly soap operas during the day. They were not appropriate for kids but we were not aware of that. We also watched talk shows and sitcoms. We pretty much watched every episode of our favourite shows that summer. My English naturally improved.

"Nila, come with me," said Ruby one day, coming up to me as I was sitting on our bedroom floor playing with my doll. I had no clue what she was leading me to. We went into our parents' bedroom and walked over to the bed. "Look," she said. Ruby lifted the mattress slightly at the head and pulled out some folded papers. She began to unfold them one by one. They had pictures of white women posing in bikinis. I tried to read the descriptions. "Sexy Girl," I said out loud. What does that mean? I thought. "*Az baba's*," It's father's, Ruby confirmed with a smirk. She had found his hidden stash of pictures of bikini models which our mother would probably be very upset about. It felt like a bad idea from the start to follow Ruby. She was always getting herself into trouble and now she had put me in a dangerous situation.

"*Kooja astain?*" Where are you guys? we heard him shout loudly. My father had heard us talking, while he was taking his nap on the living room couch. We realized we had woken him, and he was on his way towards us. I froze with panic trying to figure out where I could escape. I bolted out at the speed of light to Abdullah's bedroom and hid under his bed before my father entered the hallway. I could see his feet in the hallway as he looked for us. He was obviously angry at us for being too loud. I had no idea where Ruby was hiding but I knew she was not that quick at thinking. He walked over to his bedroom and I knew he was going to find those papers sticking out from his mattress.

Then I began hearing Ruby screaming and crying. Father had found her hiding in his bedroom and knew it was she who had gone through his private stuff. I rushed out from under Abdullah's bed and ran out of the front door apartment into the hallway to ask anyone for help but it was empty. I ran down the hallway to see if I knew any neighbours, but I was too scared to knock and speak to strangers. I ran back into the apartment and could still hear Ruby screaming. I opened his bedroom door and he had her on the bed with her back open again as he beat on it. His hands were big and strong. Her back was already red and her face was pouring with tears and spit. "*Nako! Nako!*" I screamed for him to stop and said that I was going to call for help. He stopped for a second and said that I didn't need to but then started beating her again. I grabbed the phone and started pressing 9-1-1. I didn't understand the person who was asking questions so I hung up and called my mother's friend. She was an Afghan woman so I was able to ask for help. *"Baba mayzana Ruby! Baba mayzana Ruby!"* Father is beating Ruby! Father is beating Ruby! I screamed. My father burst into the living room, grabbed the phone and hung it up. *"Keera zang zadee?"* Who did you call? he asked angrily. Then a few seconds later, the phone began to ring. My father told me to pick it up and tell them everything was okay. I picked up the call, "Hello?" It was the police returning my call. "Hello, someone called us, is everything all right?" a woman asked. "Yes. Accident," I replied. My father was staring down at me to make sure I answered appropriately. "All right, please be careful," she responded. "Okay. Bye," I said and hung up immediately. My father was catching his breath and sat down in disbelief that I actually knew how to call the police on him. My father knew that beating your children was a crime here.

I walked away and went straight to Ruby. She was crying helplessly from the pain. I pulled her up and we hid in our bedroom. Mother found out about what happened because her friend had informed her. At first, she didn't believe what was going on, but then when I showed her Ruby's back, she realized that we were not lying. Ruby's back was red with bruising from the last two beatings. Mother then spoke to father. He began yelling about how much trouble Ruby was causing. Mother was absolutely unaware of what we were going through. She used to make a joke about how serious he was but there was nothing funny about being under his supervision as children. He was losing himself and needed mental help. Mother did not know what to do and there was no easy help at the time for women like her. She ended up warning him.

Father became more abusive but this time more towards mother. As his depression and despair over his future and independence became worse, he became toxic towards everyone. I could hear their fights during the night about why he could not keep a job for more than a month and how the government kept threatening to not support them if he continued to not work. Father had gone through three different jobs already. Each one had ended with some argument about his disrespectful boss, poor pay, or the exploitative work conditions. Father was too old, disabled, and frail at this point to be providing for a family or to be tolerating abuse anymore but there was no financial support for his disability. The constant pressure, failures, and humiliation was bringing him down more each day. He went from a bakery dishwasher to a meat factory worker to a convenience store cashier. I remember him complaining about the bakery boss giving him the most difficult pots and pans to wash. His boss would yell at him about how slow he was and how he should not stop until it was his break. His job at the meat factory did not last more than a few days. His feet were hurting and when he took off his shoes to relieve them, the boss insulted him in front of everyone. His treatment as a man in the world was becoming more undignified. His job as a cashier was in a very rough part of the city, and after a few weeks of working, he was robbed at gunpoint and ended up with a black eye. He had tried to stop the armed robber, which could have cost him his life that night. The police officer told him he was wrong to fight back and should have just given the robber the money. I remember seeing him that early morning with a black eye from his nightshift. We could have lost our father over a few dollars.

His behaviour was becoming worse, and he was verbally abusive towards mother even in public. He would lose his temper when they were on errands, and start screaming and threatening, raising his hand as if to strike. My mother would go silent in humiliation and fear. Clearly his mental health was worsening, but there was no support for him. He would now lock himself up in his room for days and mother would tell us to stay out of his way. She explained that he missed his life in Afghanistan, where he had been a man of means, a man respected and supporting his family. He began to grow a beard. He began to look older. I could see the grey in his mostly black beard. Slowly he was losing himself. The fights at night between him and mother were painful to hear. He would insult her all of the time even though she was struggling and sacrificing because he could not support us. By the end of the fight, he would leave the apartment and disappear for a few days.

One day, mother and I were on the bus on the way home from doing errands. Ruby and Abdullah were at home and Laila at daycare. I loved to look out the window to observe the community. And then suddenly the worst sight that could ever fall upon my eyes happened. The bus stopped and I saw a man sitting inside the bus stop bench. He had a pakol on, a traditional Afghan hat. I looked at him more because of how strange it seemed. He had a grey blanket over his lap. He did not look like he was waiting for a bus but like someone living in the bus shelter. He had a bag beside him. His hands were joined behind his head, which was tilted back. I stared at him a bit more to catch his eyes. He pushed his head up and started staring out at the road. I looked at him closer and I recognized my father. "Baabaaaa!" I screamed through the window trying to get his attention, beating with my hands against it. "Baba!" He was homeless and living on the streets and mother had not told us. Now he was right in front of me. Mother turned around to see what I was crying about. We were now both in disbelief. Father did not hear or notice me and the bus was leaving the stop. I kept screaming his name to get him to notice and come with us. Mother grabbed my hands and sat me down, her arms tight around me. "*Shup baush. Shup baush.*" Be quiet, be quiet, she said as the other passengers stared to see what was going on.

What had happened to my father? Why was he living on the streets like this? I cried uncontrollably. He had not only abandoned us, but he had also abandoned himself. I could not recognize him anymore. I had lost the father who had carried me across the border from Afghanistan, who would always defend me against my older siblings, the father who had brought us our first TV, who had danced most beautifully when my sister Laila was born in Islamabad. I missed the father who brought mother home from the hospital in Islamabad and looked after her. He was gone. He was now someone else and somewhere else. My father died for me in that moment. He was a stranger I did not know or understand anymore. Was he happier in the streets than with his own family? Had he given up on us? How was he going to survive the winter like this? I still worried and cared for him. Mother never told us what was happening with father. She did not explain where he was or what he was doing while he was away. Now I knew. The world had shown me a cruel sight. The world had again shown me it had no mercy. It was loss after loss for us.

I kept the secret to myself and did not tell my siblings. It was shameful to share and horrible to accept. Then one day, just like the moon and sun, the truth came out. "*Babait mayra pass Afghanistan,*" Your father is going back to Afghanistan, she told us. We all looked at each other in dismay. We could do nothing but drop our heads down and cry. Our father was far from perfect but at one point in time he was for us. We knew him at his best and then at his worst. No words could come out of our mouths. We could only try to keep breathing and swallow the painful realization. We all knew something bad was coming but hoped it would not. We hoped for a miracle. We hoped it was not true. We hoped that time would heal us. However, our father couldn't handle who he was becoming and what he had to be in this country. He probably couldn't face the damage he had done to his wife and children. I lost my voice to ask my mother any questions and remained quiet.

Abdullah had trouble managing his emotions; he got up cursing and walked away to the kitchen. Then suddenly we heard the sound of dishes falling and breaking on the floor.

Abdullah had lost control. My mother cried and screamed at him to stop. "*Dostit daura. Dostit daura,*" He loves you, He loves you, she cried, trying to tell him to not take it as rejection of him. Ruby and I just stood watching our mother try her best to be strong for all of us. Abdullah stormed out of the kitchen and left the apartment. My mother was sitting on the kitchen chair in tears with broken dishes scattered under her. This was another circumstance to survive. Just another day of survival.

The summer was dark, and we had a lot to move forward from and leave behind. My mother wanted us to have our own new beginning and chapter. By the end of the summer, we were offered a four-bedroom subsidized townhouse rental which was out of the city and in the calm northern suburb of York.

York, Ontario

Fall 1996-1998

JUST LIKE WITH MY father, I did not get a chance to say goodbye to my teachers and friends. However, I had at least good final memories to remember them with. I would recall Play Day, my favourite day of the school year besides Pancakes with Santa. In the last week of school, a day was set aside for fun water games. We got to wear our bathing suits and splash around in the field. Water slides had been set up for us with hoses at each side. It was one of the most fun days of my life. For Pancakes with Santa, mother didn't pay for me to participate, but I made sure to attend anyway by getting to school as early as possible. They had Santa come to our school before it started so we could have pancakes with him. I remember walking into the gym and spotting Santa Claus. He was way up in the front, seated, waving as he ate his pancakes. It was the first time I had ever met Santa Claus. I wasn't allowed to go up to him because I didn't have a ticket, but being in the same room with him made me feel special enough. I sat at the bench watching the other children and their parents participate. Everyone was so jolly and cheerful. I didn't get pancakes but at least I enjoyed spending breakfast with

Santa. If it weren't for Ms Peace and my school events, I would have had a very difficult first year in Canada. I had some bad days at school, since not all the teachers were like Ms Peace, but it gave me great memories to leave the city of Toronto with. Even the mayor had visited us and told us about his cool black limousine, the kind he had always wanted as a kid. In my darkest moments that summer, I would think back to these fun memories and it would bring light back into my wounded heart.

We had spent the whole day helping to bring as much stuff down as possible to the lobby for the movers. I had not realized how much stuff my mother had hoarded. The neighbours were complaining about all the stuff taking up space and waiting in the lobby all day. One man passing us called it junk. It was mean but there was some truth in it, my mother had become a hoarder and took everything she could with us.

Mother was now taking us to our house for the first time. We were all very interested to see this big house that she kept talking about. She had already visited it with her friend and now it was ready for us to move into. Abdullah was pessimistic about the move. He had to leave behind his best friend. Abdullah and I had both enjoyed our school and community. However, I was ready for this new chapter, whereas he was having major attachment issues. I had a lot of bad memories in that apartment and did not want to be reminded of them every day. The atmosphere there had become sad and painful, but Abdullah would not let go of the past. And so it was not fun sitting in the back of the car with him moping because the pessimism was starting to rub off on me. I started to worry that this new chapter was a bad idea and would never be as good as the past. Once we arrived inside with all of our stuff, Abdullah began to scream and cry. Mother left us alone for a bit to run some errand with a friend so we were in the dark house with a bunch of boxes and Abdullah crying. Then Ruby, Laila, and I began to cry too. We all started crying together like a confused bunch of lost kids. We let Abdullah's negativity overcome us. It was hard not to—he was the oldest and supposed to be the leader now that father was gone. And here he was complaining what a bad idea this was. I became scared and cried for much of the night. By the time mother returned, we had all fallen asleep in tears.

We woke up in the morning to mother making us breakfast for the first time in a long time. She had set up the dining table on her own and boiled us some eggs. She looked cheerful and grateful. She had even decorated the eggshells with our initials on them. I was happy to see her happy and especially to be pampered by her. I very much needed it after the sad evening we had had. Abdullah was the last one down for breakfast in the morning and his mood was still bitter. He had a frown on his face and his eyes were still red from crying. He sat down aggressively and ignored us. Mother looked at him with dismay. She had worked so hard these past few weeks to turn everything around for us for the better. I knew she wanted some gratitude from us. I looked at my mother and said thank you with as much appreciation in my expression as I could, hoping that was enough confirmation that she was doing great.

After we were done with breakfast, mother had us sort the boxes out with her. Most of the stuff we took down to the basement and I wondered why she was even keeping it in the first place. She had way too many old lamps, table decorations, frames, and tables, and so on. We ended up having an entire corner of the basement with boxes full of objects. I did not even know where she had got them from. I just understood this as mother having trouble with letting things go and feeling like she might need them or sell them someday. Finally, when we were done putting things where they belonged, the house was ready to be lived in. I was not a fan of the furniture or the curtains we ended up with, but my mother's home décor ideas were antiquated. Any spot she could fill in, she would fill with something.

Abdullah was turning twelve next month. That was something to look forward to. I hoped my mother would be able to celebrate the birthday with a cake with sprinkles and cream—it was still the best part of birthdays for me. I tried just to focus on enjoying the days in our new town-house before I started school again, a new one.

I was a bit scared about how I would be treated at the new school. The neighbourhood was very different from my old one, which had lots of buildings around it with many new immigrant families like us. This new community consisted mostly of houses and looked very private. I rarely saw people come out of their homes, some of which looked like no one was ever inside. The weather began to get cold again, and I did not have much choice for jackets. Mother found me a bronze-coloured wool coat which made me look like very odd. I liked the posh feel of it but knew this was not the kind of coat other children were wearing. I felt very uncomfortable and out of place in it, but that was all mother had for me.

After a couple of weeks, mother was finally ready to walk me over to the school nearby to register me. It was about a twenty-minute walk through a residential neighbourhood, just like the walk to my old school. I naturally began to compare the new school with the old one. Abdullah's feelings had influenced me, and like him I was stuck even more in the past, which I thought was a better one. We came up to a large school at the end of our path and went up a long flight of concrete stairs to get to the entrance. Once inside, I knew we were in the wrong place. The kids looked big, and I could not see any who could be my age. They stared at us. I felt insecure about my jacket and embarrassed. Eventually, someone helped us to the office where we found out that we were in a middle school for which I was too young. The office lady gave us directions to the elementary school, which was just next door. We quickly left as mother was running out of time. We then entered the correct school and had me registered. The office lady here asked my mother if she wanted me to begin today, but I looked straight at her with a clear indication from my facial expression that the answer was a big no from me. I was scared and felt unready. Mother said she would take me home with her and I would start tomorrow. Now that we were familiar with the schools, she was also going to bring Abdullah and Ruby the next day.

My first day was pleasant. My second-grade teacher was an Indian lady with a gentle voice like Ms Peace, but she was much younger. She wore a lovely black skirt, white blouse, and black heels. I loved the way she dressed and her hairstyle too. She had black hair that was even straighter and darker than mine and hung perfectly sharp at chin length. My class was on the second floor and the students were mostly white except for one black girl and one brown girl. My teacher's name was Ms Gula and she was lovely, but she still wasn't my old teacher and this still wasn't my old school so I wasn't thrilled. Ms Gula introduced me to the class after she had sat me at my desk. Everyone greeted me and I smiled shyly. It was a bit overwhelming having everyone stare at me and not knowing any of them. The number of students seemed much bigger than at my old school. Later Ms Gula sat us down in a circle on the carpet. She asked me to talk about myself so the others could get to know me. The first thing that came out of my mouth was "In my old school." I knew that this was going to be a bad habit. Ms Gula nodded at me to continue. "In my old school, we have Play Day. It's so much fun," I said. The other students were interested to know more so I began to explain what it was. I basically made it clear to my teacher that I missed my old school and that nothing was going to compare to it. Ms Gula said, "Well let's focus on your new school and making some new memories. Okay?" I nodded but I knew my class was not going to hear the end about my old school.

My classmates were a bit odd, but I managed to make a friend named Sarah. She told me her name meant Princess in Hebrew and she was Jewish. She proudly showed me the Jewish star pendant around her neck. She was very proud of her heritage and would explain to me about the country her parents were from. "Open your planner. I will show you where it is," she said. I opened my planner, and she began to look for the map. "Here! There it is. That's Israel," she said and pointed to a very small circle.

"It is very tiny," I said. The country was a little circle in the middle of another one named Palestinian Territories. I was quite confused how or why that was possible. "Are you Arab?" she asked me with some concern. "No, I am Afghan," I quickly replied. "Okay! Good! I can't be your friend if you were Arab. My parents told me that those people are trying to kill us all the time." I was even more confused and uncomfortable. Would she not be my friend if I were Arab? Would her parents hate me if we were friends? I had no idea about this history, so I was hurt and taken aback by her question. It was unfair. I wasn't even sure what Arab meant or if I might be considered Arab. I was scared to say yes, so I just left the conversation there.

When recess came, Sarah ran up to me to play with her in the playground. I stared at her blankly and said I would like to just walk around. I ended up not fitting in with any of the girls in my class. They were quite forceful about friendship and tried to pull me into their agendas. It was like they were guilting me to be their friend. Unlike them, I had not started kindergarten at the school; most of them already had their close-knit group of friends that they grew up with. I did not feel comfortable in any of the groups. When lunch came, Sarah invited me to sit with her at a table of mostly Jewish girls. They all had brought wonderful lunches, but mine was cold, soggy chicken nuggets and fries that my mother had put in a plastic sandwich bag, and I was embarrassed of it. "What do you have for lunch?" Sarah giggled, "What is it?" She noticed I was hiding it under the table in my bag. "Chicken nuggets with fries," I replied, "but I am not very hungry right now." "Okay," she shrugged and then looked away, pulling out the rest of her well-packed lunch. "This is Nila," she pointed me to her friend beside her. "Hi," her friend waved. I smiled and tried to sneak into my mouth as much of my lunch as possible because I was very hungry.

Once the day was over, I was glad to be done. The school and community made me feel very alone even though Ms Gula was very sweet and helpful. I could not make a friend that I could relate to or who was genuinely kind towards me. I was now rightfully missing my old school and friends. Abdullah was right, I thought. This change was not good. I wanted to go back to my old life.

I kept to myself at school as the days went by. I was becoming a bit of a loner, but it was the smartest decision I could have made for myself. Anything else would have been forced. I was using all my strength not to lie just to fit and blend in. I would rather stand and walk around alone during recess since no one bothered me while I did so. Abdullah was in the middle school and Ruby was moved to a special school for students with similar needs as her.

"Nila!" my mother shouted from downstairs, "*Bya naan bukho!*" Come eat food!, she called out. The government didn't harass my mother as much about finding a job or working, now that she was the sole parent at home and needed to take care of us. She looked more rested, relaxed, and in her element. Now she just wanted to put her health and family first. I was glad to see her finally at home. But the challenges weren't really ending. Abdullah and Ruby continued to have their own problems at school. Ruby hated her alternative school, which was located in an isolated part of town, and to which she had to take a small school bus with other students with special needs like her. Abdullah was not focused on schoolwork but in becoming the leader of his gang of new friends. It seemed that Abdullah compensated his weakness at school by having a popular, cool personality. His social skills were amazing, so that was where he focused his attention. He made friends easily, scared a lot of people, and had everyone wanting to be like him.

A few months living in our new house went by peacefully, we were busy with adjusting to our new schools and routines. Mother was very focused on Laila starting junior kindergarten and on Ruby because of the trouble she was having at her new school. It was very small, with only five students in her class who had behaviour issues. Everyday there was some kind of complaint, that she was running off, getting into fights, or not listening to the teachers. I could not blame Ruby for not adjusting—the school was even more socially isolating, and they had prescribed medication for her to take. It was like watching a train wreck in progress, how the school and professionals handled her needs as a child. It was all very new, dealing with students with needs like hers. Their approach to separate them from regular school and kids made Ruby feel worse as a child, not better. She felt more left out, strange, and bored by this little class and school in the middle of nowhere.

One day Ruby's school called my mother about Ruby attempting to cut herself at her desk with a kitchen knife and telling her teacher that she wished she were dead. Because she was deemed as suicidal and self-harming, she was examined again and prescribed more, stronger medication. They then transferred her to a school even farther away that was in an entirely different city because they supposedly could provide her with better support. Ruby would ask my mother what she would do if she killed herself, mother would look her right in the eyes and say, I would run into the road and kill myself too if you did. Ruby looked terrified by how confident and crazy my mother sounded in her answer. I knew this had an effect on her and was keeping her from really harming herself. My mother was now busier, keeping up with Ruby's appointments, so Abdullah and I were pretty much on our own when it came to school. That year went by with me having one consistent friend, an Indian girl in my class named Pooja. We were not the best of friends but we both cared about doing well in school and didn't care about being popular. She would share her lunch with me when I had none and helped me do better with class work.

Now that mother was home with us, the summer looked a lot different. Mother encouraged us to spend it at home reading as many books as possible. She took us to the library where we got our library cards and a bag full of books for each of us. I spent most of the summer in my bedroom reading comics and a novel series while mother focused on Ruby. Abdullah was becoming more rebellious and staying out late with the neighbourhood kids. My mother lost track of what he was up to and doing with his life. Abdullah was now a teenager and was becoming rougher with his circle of friends. That summer I did not see him much, but my mother was worried every night about what he was up to. He began to stay at his friends' homes for days and stay locked up in his room when he was home. When school began that year, he dropped out after the first month. He knew he was failing his classes and saw no point in trying. He also could not afford anything he wanted for himself so wanted to make some money. Mother was devastated by his decision and fought with him every day to go back to school. She told him she would buy him his favourite sneakers that he always wanted but that was not enough. Abdullah knew mother didn't have the money to pay for expensive things for us. Their fights pushed him further away and one day he left with most of his clothes, to stay at one of his friends. We didn't know much about his friends but that they were mostly drop-outs as well, some of them having been in and out of juvenile detention. I tried to find out what Abdullah was up to from the neighbourhood kids, but they would just say he was really cool and making money selling stuff on the streets.

As if mother did not have her hands full with a toddler and the special needs of Ruby, we got a call from the police that they had arrested Abdullah for assaulting a teacher. Supposedly, Abdullah was at his old school waiting for a friend from summer school when a teacher approached and asked him to leave the property, where he was smoking. Abdullah shoved the teacher and punched him. The teacher pressed charges against him and Abdullah was now at a juvenile detention centre awaiting trial. Mother took Ruby and me to visit him. The building looked like a school with no windows, but the single door to enter was of heavy metal that unlocked on its own. When we got inside, the workers told us that we would only be able to see him from behind a glass partition. We sat at a little booth with space for only one person to sit. Ruby and I stood behind our mother as she waited for him to come out. Surprisingly, Abdullah was smiling when he came out and happy to see us. He explained that he would be out in a month and they were just holding him temporarily. He reassured mother that the other boys in there were good with him. Mother was strong that day and did not cry at all. Abdullah made her feel that everything was going to be fixed and he promised to be back home.

A couple of weeks went by before Abdullah was released. However, the happiness of his return did not last long, for he was arrested again for an even worse charge—possession of an unregistered gun. Abdullah explained to us that it was not his and the owner was an adult who placed it quickly in his bag when the police pulled up on the group that he was hanging out with. When the police checked his bag, Abdullah took the charge and wouldn't snitch on the adult. Abdullah was back in the detention centre and this time to serve at least a year in detention and another in house-arrest. Mother was devastated by the news but was happy he was alive and she could visit him. That's what kept her going. We would visit him almost every weekend that year until he was finally released into house-arrest with a monitor around his ankle. Mother's focus was on him staying home and being home before his curfew. She was split between keeping Ruby and Abdullah alive. They both were showing their risky behaviour at the same time. I chose to just stay to myself and prevent adding anymore stress on mother.

"Nila!" mother screamed at the top of her lungs. It was late at night and I was about to fall asleep. I pulled myself out of bed quickly and ran downstairs to my mother, who was screaming at the front door, where stood two police officers. One was a woman who tried to help pick mother up from the floor. The police were familiar with Abdullah and knew where he lived. They had sent officers over to inform us that he had died at a crime scene from multiple stab wounds. He was past his curfew leaving a bar when someone in the parking lot got into a fight with him. My mother was broken into pieces on the floor having difficulty breathing at this news of his murder. He was just fourteen years old. He did not deserve it, he was deeply scarred, hurt, and lost here without our father. I did not have a moment for myself to take in what was happening. My mother needed me right now. All I could remember was the good memories I shared with Abdullah when we were much younger in Kabul. I could see his smile and hear his laugh. The best memories we had were from years ago playing in the wheat field. So much had changed since then. There was no Kabul. There was no farm. There was no father. And now there was no Abdullah. There were only dreams of Kabul and of us there. Our family had been torn by the war in so many ways. We had gone from a family of six to now of four within a handful of years. Life was changing so fast and hurting us so badly. Where was mercy? I still had seen none of it.

I now had more images of blood and violence added to my memory. In between the moments of remembering him smiling would be images of him bleeding to death on a cold pavement all alone.

The world would not let me enjoy beauty. There was nothing left besides prayer and poetry to cope with the pain. I was now ten years old, full of a lifetime of tragedy.

At his funeral, I read a poem in memory of him, of us, of our childhood as Afghan children:

Does it make sense
that even when surrounded by beauty,
I cannot stop the bleeding
and cries that project from it?

I add beauty to my life
but I still cannot stop the pain
and screams of the world.
You cannot be a blissful flower
when you've grown
with the reminders of endless violence.
I am a bleeding garden.